"Hi,

Jeff laughed as he said those words, somehow believing Diane would understand his little joke as he walked inside the kitchen.

That belief disappeared when a loaf of bread flew through the air and plopped against his face—courtesy of Diane.

"Do you know what everyone in town is saying? They think we're sleeping together. They think I'm trying to catch you. Everyone in the grocery store thinks I'm a kept woman!"

Which explained her reaction to his teasing. "Ah. I guess my words weren't too funny, huh?"

"Oh, you were hysterical," she replied, slight tears in her eyes. "Aren't you worried about what everyone thinks is going on here?"

"No. I mean, we're both adults, single. If people want to believe we're—" He broke off, unable to even talk about sleeping with Diane without reacting to the thought.

"Pretty soon they'll be expecting wedding bells!" Diane exclaimed with a groan.

Jeff felt a groan coming on himself. Because the thought of Diane and him and wedding bells wasn't creating the same reaction at all....

Dear Reader,

This month, Harlequin American Romance delivers your favorite authors and irresistible stories of heart, home and happiness that will surely leave you smiling.

TEXAS SHEIKHS, Harlequin American Romance's scintillating continuity series about a Texas family with royal Arabian blood, continues with *His Shotgun Proposal* by Karen Toller Whittenburg. When Abbie Jones surprised Mac Coleman with the news of her pregnancy, honor demanded he give her his name. But could he give his shotgun bride his heart?

Another wonderful TOTS FOR TEXANS romance from bestselling author Judy Christenberry is in store for you this month with *Struck by the Texas Matchmakers*, in which two children in need of a home and several meddling ladies play matchmakers for a handsome doctor and a beautiful lawyer. Harlequin American Romance's theme promotion, THE WAY WE MET...AND MARRIED, about marriage-of-convenience romances, begins this month with *Bachelor-Auction Bridegroom* by Mollie Molay. And old passions heat up in Leandra Logan's *Family: The Secret Ingredient* when Grace North's first crush, now a single father, returns to town with his precocious little girl and ends up staying under the heroine's roof.

Enjoy this month's offerings and come back next month for more stories guaranteed to touch your heart!

Wishing you happy reading,

Melissa Jeglinski
Associate Senior Editor
Harlequin American Romance

JUDY CHRISTENBERRY

Struck by the Texas Matchmakers

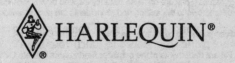

HARLEQUIN®

TORONTO • NEW YORK • LONDON
AMSTERDAM • PARIS • SYDNEY • HAMBURG
STOCKHOLM • ATHENS • TOKYO • MILAN • MADRID
PRAGUE • WARSAW • BUDAPEST • AUCKLAND

ISBN 0-373-16878-0

STRUCK BY THE TEXAS MATCHMAKERS

Printed in U.S.A.

ABOUT THE AUTHOR

Judy Christenberry has been writing romances for fifteen years because she loves happy endings as much as her readers. A former French teacher, Judy now devotes herself to writing full-time. She hopes readers have as much fun reading her stories as she does writing them. She spends her spare time reading, watching her favorite sports teams and keeping track of her two daughters. Judy's a native Texan, but now lives in Arizona.

Books by Judy Christenberry

HARLEQUIN AMERICAN ROMANCE

*4 Brides for 4 Brothers
†Tots for Texans

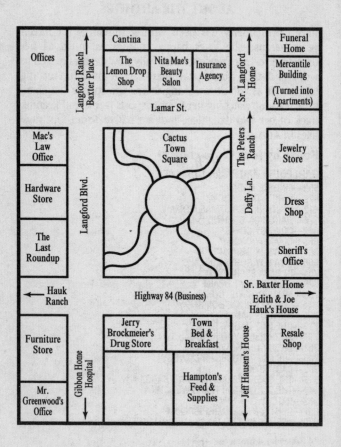

Chapter One

She'd hoped this day would never come.

Diane Peters shook herself, determined not to think in those terms. After all, most people would consider her to be a lucky woman.

Fresh out of law school, she'd just been offered a position with the most prestigious law firm in the area.

The area of Cactus, Texas.

It wasn't that she didn't like Cactus. It was her hometown, and she had a lot of good memories from her childhood. Her family had never been wealthy, but they'd been happy. She and her five brothers and sisters had shared adventures and laughter.

When she was thirteen, however, her father had died suddenly. Her mother had been a great cook and housekeeper, a devoted wife and mother. But she was a disaster as a breadwinner.

Diane sighed as she slowed down for the curve in the narrow road that led to her childhood home.

Suddenly she threw on her brakes. A car rested half in the ditch, half on the road, the driver side crushed.

Diane frowned. The car hadn't been there when she'd driven by an hour ago. As she slowed to a stop, a small face appeared at the back window.

A child? Someone was in the car? She slammed her old Volkswagen sedan into Neutral, pulled up the handbrake and jumped out of the car. Then she ran for the other vehicle.

"Are you all right?" she cried before she even got to the car.

The toddler, whose face she'd seen from the road, pressed her face against the glass, smearing it with big, fat tears.

Diane wanted to cuddle the baby to her, but she saw the other two occupants. The fact that the driver and the little boy in the back seat weren't moving made them her first priority.

Without opening the car door, she called, "Just a minute, baby," before she turned around and ran back to her car to find the cell phone her sister Katie and her husband, Gabe, had given her. Thank God.

She dialed Doc's number, grateful she still remembered it.

"Doctor's office."

"This is Diane Peters. There's been a wreck on FM 29. A lady and two children are hurt. I don't know what to do. Can Doc come?"

"We'll get help to you. Have you called the sheriff's office?"

"No, I—"

"We'll call for you. Help should be there soon."

The click in her ear reminded Diane to move. She tossed the cell phone into her front seat and rushed back to the car. The driver door wouldn't open. The back door, though slightly damaged, did open partially after she tugged on it for several minutes.

The toddler grabbed for her.

Diane's first inclination was to hold the baby, but she left her buckled in the car seat to see if she could help the others. The lady driver was unconscious. She'd bled quite a lot, but the bleeding appeared to have stopped. Diane felt helpless. She could quote laws, but she knew nothing about serious injuries.

She turned her attention to the little boy. Reaching across the child seat, she touched his denim-clad leg. "Are you awake?" she asked.

He stirred but the only response was a moan. She didn't see any blood, however, so she didn't know anything else to do. She'd read that moving an injured person could cause more problems. Since it was summer in Cactus, she didn't even have a jacket she could use to help prevent shock.

"Mama, Mama!" the little girl cried, trying to cling to Diane.

She managed to release the clasp holding the child in place and lifted the little girl into her arms. "There, sweetie, it's going to be all right."

She hoped she was telling the truth, but she prayed Doc would get there soon. The older gentleman was such a comfort, always seeming to know what to do.

As she cuddled the little girl against her, she heard the sound of a car speeding toward them. "Please let that be Doc," she prayed, moving to the edge of the road.

She was disappointed when it came into view. Doc drove an old red pickup. This vehicle was a navy blue Suburban. Cactus was too small to be able to afford paramedics and all the emergency equipment of big cities. But maybe the driver would stop anyway. She waved and relief flooded her when he braked to a stop. At least she wouldn't be alone anymore.

"Is she hurt?" the man asked briskly almost before he was out of the car.

"Not badly, I think. Not like the other two," she said. "The doctor is on the way, but—"

"I'm the doctor," he snapped, not slowing as he hurried to the car.

Diane stared after him, shocked. Doc was no longer in Cactus? Surely he hadn't died. Katie or her mother would've told her. But then they hadn't said he'd moved away either. She knew about Samantha, Mac Gibbons's wife, who had come to Cactus to be Doc's partner, but—

"Come help me," he ordered.

Diane hurried over, still dealing with the surprise.

"Set the little one on the grass and help me get the boy out. He's got a broken arm and I don't want to do more damage than I have to."

It was difficult to free herself from the toddler sobbing in her arms, but she promised she'd be right back with her brother. Then she hurried to help the doctor.

"Can you manage to handle his legs? He's heavier than he looks."

Diane didn't waste time telling him she'd been raised on a farm and had helped pay for college working at the airport as a ticket agent which included shifting luggage. She nodded.

Gently they transferred the boy to the patch of grass where his sister was sobbing.

"Stay with them and hold his arm against his body until I can stabilize the woman."

Before Diane could agree, he'd disappeared into the car again. But she wasn't complaining. She was relieved the man seemed to know what he was doing. Sitting down on the grass, not caring about any grass stains on her new dress, she let the little girl snuggle into her lap while she gently held the little boy's arm against his chest.

"Shh, baby, you're all right," she comforted.

She felt more sure of that when she heard the siren that meant someone from the sheriff's office was on the way. She hoped it was Cal Baxter, the sheriff himself.

By the time the Blazer halted, the doctor was beside it. Diane saw Cal get out. He nodded in her direction, taking in the children, before the doctor urged him back to the wreck.

The boy moaned and his eyes fluttered open.

"Be still, honey, the doctor's helping your mama right now," Diane said, hoping the words would help him, but they only reminded her smallest charge that she didn't have her mama. Which, of course, brought on renewed sobbing.

More sirens sounded. Diane was startled as an ambulance appeared. She hadn't realized Cactus had an emergency vehicle.

By the time the ambulance came to a halt, Cal and the new doctor had gotten the woman out of the car. The ambulance driver brought out a stretcher and they placed the woman upon it and moved her straight to the ambulance.

As soon as she was put inside, Cal pulled out his cell phone. "Tell Sam the patient's on her way. Here's Jeff to give you the details." He handed the phone to the doctor and came to Diane's side.

"Hello, Diane. Need some assistance?"

"Yes, please," she said. "The doctor said to keep the boy's arm still and this little lady is upset."

Cal reached for the little girl. With two little ones of his own, he knew how to handle them. Diane shifted the boy's head into her lap and cuddled him against her, hoping her body heat would help him. She brushed his brown hair off his face and dropped a kiss on his brow.

The doctor reached them with a blanket under his arm and Cal asked, "Did the lady come to?"

The man shook his head and knelt beside Diane. "How's he doing?"

"He seems to be in a state of shock," she said quietly.

The doctor spread the blanket over the little boy.

Doc, he'd met Katie...and been attracted to her, in spite of his intentions.

Gabe, however, had rushed his beloved Katie to the altar to stake his claim. The Peters family, Katie's family, was large, but Diane and Raine had remained in Lubbock, the nearest large city, except when they returned for Katie's wedding.

"How badly hurt is their mother?"

Her question jolted him. He realized they'd reached the back of his Suburban. He laid his end of the stretcher on the floorboard and climbed in. The racks he'd had installed to hold a stretcher would come in handy.

"Bad," he muttered in answer.

Once the boy was settled, he climbed back out.

"Do you want me to stay back here with him, or ride with the little girl?"

"The baby," he replied. "She's getting hysterical and this little guy should be all right until we get there."

She nodded and hurried around to the back door where the baby was screaming.

The immediate lowering of the sirenlike screams showed he'd made the right decision. He stepped to Cal's side. "You going to get some help?"

"No, probably not. I've got the woman's purse. There wasn't much in the trunk but some remnants of a picnic. Red paint on the car. I'll be back to the office shortly."

"Okay, I'm taking these two in. I imagine the

woman will need a lot of work, so I'll be tied up for a while.''

With a nod to Cal, he strode to his vehicle. "Everything okay?" he asked as he climbed in.

"Yes," Diane Peters said quietly. She was sitting as close to the baby seat as possible, but he didn't have to tell her to keep the baby buckled in. Instead, her arms were cuddling the little girl, soothing her as best she could.

He started the car and made a U-turn. Then he sped toward the clinic.

WHEN THEY REACHED Cactus, Diane saw Doc waiting for them.

His comforting presence made her feel more settled.

"You got this covered?" Dr. Hausen asked as soon as they were unloaded.

"Yeah, and Sam's getting everything ready."

Doc had always sent his more serious patients into Lubbock for treatment, but the clinic had been enlarged, and both doctors were young and well-trained.

After the other doctor had disappeared, Diane said, "Things have changed a lot since I've been gone."

"For the better. Sam and Jeff make a great team." Even as he talked, he was examining the boy. Then he asked one of the nurses to x-ray him.

"How about I check out this little angel now," he suggested, holding out his arms.

The baby had settled down as long as Diane held her. But Doc's offer didn't sit well with her. She clung to Diane's neck, her sobs starting again.

"Well, we know her tear ducts are working well," Doc said wryly. "Why don't we sit down over here," he suggested, waving to several chairs.

As she held the little girl, soothing her as much as she could, Doc listened to her heartbeat, checked her eyes and ears and felt her head.

"I think she has a mild concussion, probably a bad headache. I'm going to give her a mild sedative which should help the pain and maybe settle her down. Do you want me to have them set up a bed for her?"

Diane frowned. "Maybe I'd better continue to hold her. And keep her near her brother. She's happier when she can see him."

"You're a good girl, Diane, just like your sister. Are you staying home now?" he asked as he opened a cupboard.

Straightening her shoulders, she replied, "I'm staying." She didn't feel she had a choice. Katie had given up her dream of college when their father died and spent the next ten years putting her siblings through school. Now she was married with a new baby. It was time for Diane to take some of the burden from Katie's shoulders.

Doc paused, frowning at her over his shoulder. "You happy about that?"

"Of course. I've already been offered a job with Mac and Gabe." She worked hard at the enthusiasm.

"Since Rick Astin moved here, there's a lot more work."

"Yeah, he's made a big difference. He paid for the improvements around here, including the ambulance. Nice, isn't it?"

"Yes. It sure came in handy today." The little girl screamed when Doc approached her again, a needle in his hands.

"She's obviously been to the doctor and gotten shots before," Doc said calmly over the noise she was making. "That's good."

The nurse returned with the X rays as Doc administered the shot. By the time he'd finished examining them, the baby had subsided in Diane's arms, her lids drifting closed, her breathing becoming more even.

"Good, she's quieted down," Doc said, checking the little girl again. "We're going to set the boy's arm. Then we'll settle him into a room and you can take his sister in there, okay?"

"Sure, Doc. I'm going to call Mom while you're doing that, so she won't worry."

"Good."

Her mother was alarmed when Diane called. Gabe had called Katie after the interview, to tell her how things had gone, and she'd called their mother, so Margaret had been expecting Diane home an hour ago.

"I was so worried," she exclaimed.

"Sorry, Mom, I'm fine. But I found a wreck, with

the people injured and I came back to Cactus to help with them.''

"Oh, I'm so sorry. But you'll be home soon?''

"I don't think so. I'm holding the little girl. She's maybe two. The mother is being assessed, so I think I'll stay with the children until we know something.''

She hadn't realized she'd made a conscious decision until she'd answered her mother. But she couldn't abandon the sweetheart in her arms. Or the little boy. He couldn't be older than four. If she had children that age, she'd want—but she didn't intend to have children. She'd already made that decision.

She settled in a chair in the waiting room, asking the receptionist to let her know when they put the boy in a room. She wished she knew the children's names.

A few minutes later, Doc came and got her, escorting her and the baby to a small room with a comfortable chair near the bed.

"You sure you can stay?'' he asked.

"Yes, of course. Uh, the new doctor, is he good?''

"Very good. Why? Did he do something you didn't like?''

"No! Of course not. But I didn't know we had a new doctor, so it kind of shocked me.''

"We're lucky to have him. He was working in Houston. Came highly recommended. 'Course, he frustrates the matchmakers, you know.''

Diane noted his grin. His own wife was part of

the original group of matchmakers who had made Cactus a hotbed of romance. "What have Flo and her friends been doing?"

"Trying to find someone for the 'new' doctor to marry. You know how they are. But Jeff won't have anything to do with their attempts to elevate his social life."

"Why not?"

"He's recently widowed. Doesn't seem interested in other women."

"Oh. I'm sorry."

"Yeah. But he's a good doctor. He'll do his best for these little tykes' mother."

IN ADDITION TO A concussion, the woman had several broken ribs and a broken collarbone. Jeff, and his partner, Samantha Gibbons, spent a long time trying to put things right.

When their patient was wheeled away to recovery, Samantha sighed as she stripped off her gloves. "Good job, Jeff."

"Thanks. You, too. We work well together. That's been a joy this past year."

She smiled and nodded. "It's been a good year."

"Well, not when you were out having that little boy. At least not for me. But I've heard he's the handsomest boy in Cactus."

"You've been talking to Flo again," Samantha said with a smile.

"Or Mac."

"Or Doc. He's always treated Florence and Mac

as his family since his own wife died, but after marrying Florence, he watches over us like a hawk. And is just as prejudiced as the rest of us.''

Her smile told him she didn't object.

"Speaking of kids, I'd better check on the two little ones we brought in with her," he said, nodding in the direction the nurses had gone with the patient.

"How bad were their injuries?"

"I don't believe the little girl had much wrong with her. The boy had a broken arm and probably a concussion."

"I'll go with you," Samantha immediately said.

One of the things he liked about his partner was her dedication to her job. But with two babies of her own and a husband, he knew she was ready to go home. "I'll check on them. You go take care of your own crew."

"Thanks, Jeff. I'm hoping Flo will have cooked for us. She spoils me."

"With good reason. You've given her grandbabies. You know that's the goal of every woman in Cactus. I just wish they'd leave me alone," he added with a sigh.

"Which reminds me. I heard Diane Peters stopped to render aid. You'll have a lot in common with her soon."

"I will?" he asked, surprised. Not that he objected. He'd noticed today that she was an attractive woman, like her sister, only a little more sophisticated.

"Well, she's single and coming back to Cactus.

She'll be working with Mac as soon as she passes the bar.''

"So, the fact that we're both single is what we have in common?"

"Ah, no. The fact that both of you will be in the sights of the matchmakers is what you'll have in common." Sam paused before a big grin appeared on her lips. "Hey, maybe they'll match you two up and take care of both of you with one wedding!"

"No!" Jeff protested with more volume than he realized.

Chapter Two

Jeff could see that his adamant response to her comment had surprised Samantha.

"Are you all right?" she asked, obviously concerned about his overreaction.

"Of course," he said with a smile.

"You've been teased about the matchmakers before, but you never seemed to mind," Samantha pointed out.

"I must be tense from the surgery. It's been a little while since we've had anything so serious." He began walking toward the door, anxious to escape his friend's questions. He had an inkling about what had caused his reaction, but he certainly didn't want to think about it now.

"I'll see you tomorrow," he added as he pushed against the swinging door.

"Okay. If you need me, you'll call, won't you?"

"You know I will, Sam, but hopefully it won't be necessary."

Jeff discovered Doc waiting for him in his office.

He gave him an update on the two children and told him what room they were in. Jeff sent him home. He knew Doc's wife, Florence, would be anxious until he arrived.

He surprised himself with the wish he had someone waiting for him. He'd thought about hiring a housekeeper, but it wasn't the same thing. Besides, there was only him, and he had a woman coming in to clean once a week. And he wasn't used to home-cooked meals. His wife had been a school counselor and worked long hours. They'd usually met at a restaurant before they went home for the evening.

When he opened the door of the little boy's room, he paused before entering, staring at the picture before him.

Diane Peters sat in a large chair next to the bed, the toddler still in her arms. Diane was talking softly to the little boy who lay in the bed, his arm in a cast.

Just then, she noticed Jeff in the doorway. Her gaze fell on him and she stopped talking.

"Good evening," he said casually, strolling into the room. "How are my patients?"

The toddler snuggled closer to Diane, her gaze wide with fear. The boy's eyes were wide, too, but Jeff could see his effort to be brave. His heart went out to the child, feeling the pressure to be strong for his baby sister.

Reaching the bed, he picked up the boy's wrist on his good arm and took his pulse. "Did Doc fix up your arm, son? Are you in pain?"

The boy shook his head no. "Mama?"

His sister whimpered and Jeff watched Diane's soothing hands as she comforted the little girl.

"Your mother is just fine," he hurriedly said. "She's still asleep right now. You should be able to see her tomorrow or the day after, though."

Diane's gaze showed as much relief as the children's. He hoped she realized he'd simplified things for the children. He wasn't sure the woman would awaken that quickly. With the concussion, that couldn't be guaranteed.

"Have you introduced yourselves to Miss Peters?" he asked, in an attempt to distract them.

Both children looked confused.

Diane hurriedly said, "That's me. I told them my name is Diane," she explained to him. "And this is Toby and Janie Duncan."

He greeted the two children by name and watched them relax a little. "Do you live here in Cactus?"

The boy opened his mouth to answer, but a familiar voice behind Jeff responded instead.

"No, they live in Lubbock," Cal said. He came into the room and stopped at the end of the boy's bed. "I've called their number but there's no answer."

Diane quietly said, "Toby said their daddy died a few months ago. He doesn't remember any more family."

"Toby, is it?" Cal repeated in a kind voice. "You don't have any grandparents or aunts or uncles, Toby?"

The boy shook his head, his bottom lip trembling.

"Okay," Cal said easily. "Do you remember what happened, Toby? Today, I mean."

The boy paled and Jeff reached for his hand, hoping to offer reassurance. Diane, from the other side of the bed, reached out to touch him also.

Toby opened his mouth but no words came out. Finally, he managed, "A car, a red car, hit us."

Cal nodded and smiled again, as if Toby had given him just what he needed to hear. "Good boy. How are you feeling?"

"I think Toby's had a tough day," Jeff said, hoping Cal would understand that the children didn't need any more questioning.

"So, they're going to stay here?" Cal asked.

"For tonight," Jeff said. "The nurse is going to come with their trays. After they eat, they'll each get a sedative to help them sleep tonight. Then tomorrow, Toby, and Janie, of course, will probably be released."

"But their mother..." Diane began, then trailed off, her gaze on the little boy's face.

"Right," Cal agreed, seeming to recognize her dilemma. "We'll need to find someone to care for them until we can consider our options."

"I can take care of them," Diane offered.

Jeff looked away from her. A compassionate woman was always attractive to him. His own mother had been ill most of his life. He'd gone into medicine because of her. But she'd been unable to be the mother of storybooks or television shows.

The problem with Diane was that he was already attracted to her. When he'd seen her holding the toddler, her gaze filled with worry and not a little fear, he'd recognized that compassion, along with her natural beauty. Her strength and determination had compounded his interest and curiosity. Which explained why he'd overreacted to Samantha's teasing.

For the first time since his wife died, he was attracted to another woman.

"Um, it's a big responsibility. I can't tell you how long…if Cal doesn't find any relatives, we could be talking weeks."

As he'd expected from his experience with her at the wreck, her chin rose and she glared at him. "I'm not an idiot. I understand that. But I'm not going to work full-time at the law firm until after I take the bar exam." She turned to Cal. "Can I take charge of the kids, Cal?"

"Do you have room in your mother's house, Diane? I know Joe got his own place when he moved back, but there's still Paul and Susan at home. And you."

"If I share with Susan, the two little ones can sleep in my bedroom," she said. "It will be crowded, but I think they need to be together anyway."

"Works for me," Cal agreed.

"Is that okay with you, Toby?" Jeff asked. "Would you mind going with Diane tomorrow?

That way you'll be close to the hospital so you can see your mom.''

The little boy nodded, turning to look at Diane. "Yes, sir," he whispered.

Diane smiled tenderly at him. "Good. You'll like my home, Toby. My mom makes great cookies."

The little girl sat upright, speaking for the first time without tears. "Cookie?"

Diane hugged her with a smile. "Ah, I found something you like, didn't I, Janie?"

"I'd better have their dinners brought in. Do you mind helping feed them, Diane?" Jeff asked, already knowing the answer.

"Of course not."

He and Cal left the room together. As soon as Jeff had given instructions to a nurse, he turned to the sheriff. "Do you think she'll be able to handle the job?"

"Diane? Oh, yeah. The Peters kids are responsible. While Katie took the brunt of the burden when their dad died, they all pitched in and worked hard. Only Susan, the baby, who's a senior this year, has shown any tendencies for teenage rebellion. If Diane says she can handle the job, you can be sure she can."

Jeff sighed. "Okay."

"How long before the kids settle down for the night?"

Raising his eyebrow, Jeff said, "About half an hour. Why?"

"I thought I'd go to The Last Roundup for dinner.

I know Diane hasn't eaten since Janie hasn't left her arms. And you couldn't have had a chance, after doing the operation. I thought both of you might join me.''

Jeff searched for a reason to turn down the invitation. But he was no masochist. He had nothing at the house ready to eat, and it had been a tough day.

''I don't know about Diane, but I'll take you up on your offer.''

''Good. And I'll count on you to persuade Diane. She deserves a treat after all she did today.''

Jeff agreed that she deserved more than a steak, but he wasn't looking forward to spending more time with her. On the other hand, without the toddler in her arms, maybe he'd find her less attractive.

Right.

DIANE QUIETLY WATCHED the two children subside into sleep, grateful that for a few hours they could forget the miserable day they'd just experienced. Janie had eaten more readily than Toby. Unless she or the nurse encouraged him, he'd been reluctant to eat. Diane could see the worry in his eyes.

Janie had eaten a good meal, her young mind unable to concentrate as well as her older brother's. Fortunately, the sedative they'd given her had been in the form of a pill this evening, not a needle. She never even realized she'd been given medicine and was easily tucked into the second bed in the room.

Toby, too, took his medicine, unsuspecting that it would put him to sleep.

"I think they're really asleep now, Diane," the nurse, a woman she'd known in school, said.

"I guess you're right, Sandy. But I'm afraid they'll wake up and start crying. Janie has powerful lungs."

"I know," Sandy agreed with a quiet laugh. "I heard her."

"It's been a long day. I hope Mom saved me some dinner."

The two of them left the room, saying their good-byes. Diane insisted Sandy call her if the children needed her before morning.

Diane turned toward the exit, weariness finally hitting her. She sagged against the wall for a moment to gather her strength.

Warm, familiar hands caught her around the waist. "You all right?" Dr. Hausen asked.

She went rigid. "Yes, thank you, just—just a little tired."

"You should be exhausted. You were a great help today."

"Thank you," she murmured and moved away from him.

"I'm under strict instructions to bring you to The Last Roundup to join Cal for dinner."

Diane turned to face the man she'd only met a few hours ago. "Oh, no, I have to go home. My mother—"

"I just talked to your mother and explained that we were going to feed you before we let you go home. She agreed that would be best."

Diane wanted to sag against the wall again, but the man might decide she needed his touch, and she definitely didn't want that. Something strange came over her when he touched her. "No, thanks, I need to go home."

"And how will you get there?" he asked, his voice casual, as if he had little interest in her response.

"Why, I'll drive—my car! It's—Oh, no, I think I left the motor running! Could you take me—"

Before she could finish her request, he said, "Of course I will. After we eat. I've had a long day, too."

What choice did she have? Or what excuse to drag the doctor out for the drive to her car before he ate? "Of—of course. Will it take long? I mean, I'm afraid someone might steal my car."

"I'd bet Cal turned off the motor and took your keys. Let's go ask him."

That suggestion dismissed any of her reluctance to join Cal at the restaurant. In fact, she was hurrying along when she felt the doctor's touch on her arm.

"There's no need to run. I'm not as young as you," he told her, a rueful smile on his handsome lips.

"Sorry," she said, slowing slightly.

"You're supposed to say, 'Oh, no, doctor, you're not old.'"

Diane couldn't hold back a grin as he spoke those

words in a falsetto voice. So he had a sense of humor. A lot of men did.

"You're right. I should have said that, because it's true. But I'm afraid my mind was on my car."

"Hmm, that's the first time I've ever come in second to a dilapidated sedan."

Her cheeks burned. "My car may not be in the best condition, but it's served me well."

He seemed embarrassed, too, as if he hadn't meant to imply any competition between him and the car. "Of course, I was just teasing you. How long have you had the car?"

"My brother Joe bought it from one of his college buddies for me. It was seventeen years old then and I've driven it for six more years."

"Wow, that's impressive. And what's its name?"

She spun around to stare at him. "How did you know—I mean, it hasn't—" She was about to deny naming her car, but she couldn't lie when she looked into his blue eyes. "I named *her* Daisy," she confessed, her chin up.

He chuckled. "An appropriate name for a car that probably lived through the flower power age."

"I can assure you Daisy is a lady," she said, with just a hint of a smile.

By that time, much to Diane's surprise, they'd reached the entrance of The Last Roundup, the nicest restaurant in Cactus, on the town square. Since the owner was Cal's wife, Jessica, Diane didn't have any doubt about them getting seated at once.

When they were escorted to a table, she was surprised to discover Jessica sitting with her husband.

"Diane!" Jessica exclaimed. "I heard you were back in town, but I hadn't seen you. How are you?"

"A little tired," she replied, but she smiled.

"Cal told me about your day. And I also heard about your interview. I talked to Alex earlier today. Congratulations."

"Thanks, Jess. I guess the grapevine in Cactus is alive and well." No surprise, especially since Alex was Alexandra Langford, third partner in Mac Gibbons and Gabe's law firm, and had married Tuck, one of their best friends.

While Diane and Jess were chatting, Cal and the doctor had been talking in low voices. Since none of them had ordered, she was surprised again when a waitress arrived with a full tray.

Jessica said, "We ordered for you, since it's late and I knew you'd be hungry. You were on your way home before lunch, weren't you? So you haven't eaten since breakfast."

"I'm not the only one," Diane protested. "The doctor and Cal haven't eaten, either."

"Actually, I grabbed a sandwich while I was making some phone calls," Cal confessed, an easy grin on his face. "Jeff hasn't eaten. So we figured whatever we ordered for you, you'd fall on it. Right?"

"I'm ready," the doctor said. "And Diane, call me Jeff. People will start looking for Doc, if you don't."

"That's right," Jessica teased. "You're the young doctor."

"Or the new doctor," Jeff added. "Diane's already told me I'm old."

"No, I didn't!" Diane protested. By that time, the waitress had put all the food on the table, and everyone was distracted by the aroma. Diane tried not to look ravenous, but she soon realized no one else was paying any attention.

Some time later, Jessica leaned back in her chair, and said, "Well, I hope y'all enjoyed the food. I was hungrier than I thought."

"Me, too," Diane said, putting her last bite of steak into her mouth.

"So," Cal drawled, "tell me why you called Jeff here old."

Darn. Diane had hoped they would've forgotten Jeff's words. "I didn't. He said he was older and I forgot to deny it because I was worried about—oh! My car. Did you turn off the engine, Cal?"

"Of course. I have the keys in my pocket."

"Oh, thank you so much. The doctor said—"

"Jeff," he reminded her.

"Oh, yes, uh, Jeff said you would have."

"As soon as we have dessert, I'll run you out to your car," Cal promised.

As Diane was thanking him, Jeff interrupted. "I don't have anyone waiting at home for me, Cal. You and Jess can go home and I'll take Diane to her car."

Before Diane could protest, Cal thanked Jeff.

Then he signaled the waitress and ordered dessert. Both men opted for carrot cake, but Jessica and Diane chose the peach cobbler layered with cream cheese and topped with ice cream.

"Your sister is the reason I can't eat here that often," Jessica said as she took her first bite of cobbler. "I can resist the carrot cake, though I'm in the minority, but the cobbler is just too good."

"Katie made this?" Diane asked.

"You didn't know? She added it to the menu almost a year ago. And sold the recipe to the holding company for all the franchises. You can get this cobbler all over Texas."

"Oh, yes, I remember when she called and told us the news, but I've never eaten it."

"Katie's a wonderful cook," Jeff said.

"Yeah, but Jessica's good, too," Cal loyally added.

"No question," Jeff said. "I've never had a better steak, and Houston had a lot of good restaurants."

"You're from Houston?" Diane asked, as if Doc hadn't told her earlier. She hoped she hid her envy. Her dream of settling in a big city, getting completely away from Cactus, wasn't possible. But she found it hard to believe anyone would actually *choose* Cactus when they had that opportunity.

Jeff seemed to be concentrating on his cake, but he answered, "Yeah."

"And you chose to come here? Don't you find it, uh, dull in comparison?"

He looked up and stared at her. "No. Cactus has everything I want or need."

Jessica frowned. "Diane, don't you want to be in Cactus?"

Uh-oh. "Why, yes, of course, Jessica. I wouldn't want to live away from my family." She added a big smile to convince one of her sister's best friends.

Jessica seemed to accept her answer, and the conversation turned to more general topics, leaving Diane time to finish her dessert.

After thanking Jessica and Cal and saying goodbye, Jeff escorted Diane to his Suburban. Then they headed down the farm-to-market road where she'd left her Volkswagen, her keys in her pocket.

Jeff said nothing, and Diane appreciated his silence. She didn't want to share any personal conversation with the handsome man. He might be older than her, but he was young enough to stir some attraction if she let him.

And then he completely surprised her by abruptly asking, "Why don't you want to live in Cactus?"

Chapter Three

Diane stiffened. It was one thing for old friends to question her, but she'd just met this man. Whether she wanted to live in Cactus or not was none of his business. Still, she felt compelled to answer. "You're wrong. I'm delighted to have found a good job here in Cactus."

"Didn't sound like it to me," he muttered, not looking in her direction.

"You don't know me."

"True, but part of a doctor's job is to pay attention to what's not being said."

She stared out the window, trying to ignore him.

Which explained why she heard the sirens at once. She whipped her head around, staring over her shoulder. "That sounds like the fire truck."

When she'd left Cactus, the town had one fire truck and a volunteer group who tried to protect the town from fire. Had Rick Astin, their local millionaire, also staffed the fire department while she was gone?

"You're right," Jeff agreed with a frown, checking his rearview mirror.

The flashing lights appeared behind them and Jeff pulled to the side of the road. The truck sped by.

"What could be on fire?" Jeff muttered as he pulled back onto the road.

"Might be a field," Diane suggested. "I know we've had a lot of rain recently, but things are starting to dry out. A flick of a cigarette is all it would take."

"I hope that's it. Otherwise, there might be injuries. I'd better follow them as soon as I drop you at your car."

Since they were almost to her car, she gathered her purse, ready to get out quickly. "Thanks for the ride."

"I'll wait until you're safely in your car," he said.

"That's not necessary. I can—"

"Hurry," he said, ignoring her words.

The man irritated her, but she did as he asked. Once she was safely locked in her Volkswagen, he sped down the road in the direction the fire truck had taken.

Which also happened to be the direction of her home.

She wondered which of their neighbors was having difficulties. She knew her mother and stepfather would be there offering their assistance, so she'd probably have some time alone when she got home.

The closer she got to her house, however, the more she worried. There was a red glow that indicated the fire—and it appeared to be very close to her place.

When she turned the corner and her childhood home came into view, she discovered it couldn't be any closer. Her house was on fire.

JEFF WATCHED AS SMOKE continued to rise from the Peters's home. He'd arrived just after the fire trucks and had soon determined that everyone seemed to have gotten out okay. The firemen, however, were still battling the fire in the back part of the house.

Jeff turned to see Diane's car reach the house. The car jerked to a stop and she scrambled out, running toward the burning building, screaming, "Mom? Mom?"

He reached her and wrapped his arms around her. "Your family is safe. They're over here, Diane. Come on, I'll take you to them."

His words seemed to work magic over her. She sagged against him, no longer fighting his hold. He led her toward the woman and teenager sitting huddled together on the back of an old pickup.

"Diane!" Margaret Ledbetter shouted as soon as she saw her daughter.

Diane ran into her arms, hugging her and her younger sister. "Mom, is everyone all right? Where's Jack and Paul?"

"They're over there, fighting the fire. Dear, it started in your room. All your clothes and—everything is—oh, I'm so sorry. Jack had suggested we check the wiring for the air-conditioning unit we added, but I thought— I'm so sorry.''

He could tell Diane was fighting back tears, but she hugged her family closer. ''The important thing is that you're all safe.''

A few moments later, several cars pulled up near the house. Katie and Gabe Dawson got out of one and Katie rushed to them, comforting and hugging her mother and sisters.

Gabe approached Jeff and asked, ''Hell, how did this happen?''

''Margaret was just telling Diane that it was electrical. Something about an older air-conditioning unit they'd just installed in Diane's room.

''Damn! I should've insisted they let me install proper air-conditioning,'' Gabe said with a sigh. ''But Margaret and Jack don't want any help.''

Jeff knew Katie's bakery was doing well, and Gabe was a wealthy businessman, but people around Cactus were proud. Handouts were unacceptable except in dire straits.

Even as the two of them talked, the men who'd worked to put out the fire were packing up their equipment. Jeff and Gabe moved over to speak to them.

''Is it completely out?'' Gabe asked.

''Yeah. Jack and his boy had it under control before we even got here,'' one of the firemen said.

''Did any of you get injured?'' Jeff asked.

''I think Paul had a burn on his arm,'' the man who'd spoken earlier said.

Jeff looked for Diane's younger brother. He'd met him before, a few months back.

"Paul?" Jeff called when he spotted him. "Heard you got burned. Let me look at it," Jeff said as he made his way over to the younger man.

"Aw, it's nothing," Paul assured him.

With a smile, Jeff said, "Humor me. I'll feel better if I check you out."

Jack Ledbetter, Paul's stepfather, came over with a flashlight. "Need some light on the subject?" he asked as he turned it on.

"Yeah, thanks, Jack." After looking at the burn, Jeff said, "I'll need to treat it, Paul, and bandage it up so it won't get infected."

When Paul started to refuse, Jack said, "Don't be macho, boy. That's your throwing arm. How will you support me and your mom in our old age if you can't play football anymore?"

His accompanying grin was matched by Paul, who reluctantly surrendered himself to Jeff's care with no more resistance.

"You play football?" he asked.

"I'm on an athletic scholarship at Texas Tech. Ouch!" Paul exclaimed as Jeff touched his burn. His face was already pale, in spite of his pretence of no pain.

"He's really good," Jack bragged. "Goin' to play in the Superbowl someday."

Jeff smiled. "I'll expect free tickets in payment, of course." He led Paul to his vehicle so he could get his medical bag.

As the three of them moved away from the house, the group of women spotted them and dashed across the front yard to meet them at Jeff's truck.

"What happened? Who's hurt?" Katie demanded.

"Paul has a minor burn," Jeff said soothingly. "We're taking precautions so it won't get infected."

The babble of relieved voices and supportive pats on Paul's shoulders were interesting to Jeff. He'd moved to Cactus for several reasons. One of them was to feel connected again. He was alone, no family. The wealth of emotion this family shared was incredible.

Gabe rejoined them. "How is he?" he asked.

Paul grinned at his brother-in-law. "It's nothing much. The doc's being cautious so I won't sue." Everyone seemed to notice the slight wobble in the boy's voice.

Jeff prepared to clean the burn, wishing he didn't have such a large audience. It was going to be painful for Paul. "Son, this is going to hurt," he said in a low voice.

Diane overheard him. "Just a minute," she said softly. "Mom, you and Jack had better get what you need for the night from the house. You, too, Susan. Gabe, can you see if Paul has some clean clothes? And Katie, you'd better help Mom."

In seconds, only Diane and Paul remained with Jeff.

"Thanks, sis," Paul muttered. Then he looked at Jeff. "Okay, go ahead."

Diane helped hold her brother's arm while Jeff cleaned and covered the wound with salve. Then he began wrapping the arm in gauze. "I'm going to need to see you tomorrow, Paul, to check on this."

Though the young man was still pale, he'd kept quiet during the process. Now, he cleared his throat and said, "Sure, Doc. I'll be in tomorrow."

"I'll bring him," Diane added, her hands still comforting her brother.

"Do you want some pills for the pain?" Jeff asked.

Paul said no.

Diane said yes. Before her brother could argue, she added, "Just in case. You'll feel better if you get a good night's sleep."

Jeff took a couple of pills out of his bag and handed them to Diane. "One every four to six hours as needed." Then he asked, "Where are you going to sleep tonight?"

Diane and Paul looked at each other, but before either could speak, Katie had returned, carrying her daughter, Rachel. "She woke up," Katie announced. "How's Paul?"

"All taken care of," Jeff assured her. "We were just talking about where they would sleep tonight."

"With us, of course," Katie said, as if there was no question.

"But you only have one bedroom free, Katie," Diane said, frowning. "Mom and Jack will take that. I guess we can put Paul on the sofa, and I'll take the big chair to keep an eye on him, but—"

"I don't need anyone to watch me," Paul argued. "And I can sleep here in the barn."

"We'll manage," Katie insisted.

Jeff interrupted. "Look, I've got three bedrooms empty. You," he said, nodding to Diane, "Paul and Susan can stay with me tonight."

"Oh, no, we can't—there are other—"

"I'm sure there are," he said, agreeing with Diane's protest, "but it's late. Tomorrow you can make whatever arrangements you want."

Diane was acting like he wanted them in his home, intruding into his life, which was crazy. He liked living alone. And he wanted no part of Diane in his life. He sure didn't want to give the local matchmakers any ideas. But this was Cactus and people helped each other here.

"Are you sure you don't mind, Jeff?" Katie asked. "I'll admit life is hectic enough since Rachel was born, but if—"

"It will be fine. I'm not a good housekeeper, but the beds are comfortable. And Paul needs to get to bed."

"I'm fine," Paul insisted, but Jeff noticed he swayed as he tried to reassure his sisters.

Diane's arm went around him. "Sure you are, but we're not going to take any chances. We'll follow the doctor's orders to a T." She started leading Paul to her car.

"I can drive him," Jeff called.

"No, I'll drive," Diane insisted.

He hurriedly gave her directions to his house, since she was determined to get Paul to bed at once.

Gabe, Margaret and Jack joined the group and Katie hastily explained the sleeping arrangements. Jack offered Jeff his hand in gratitude, and Margaret hurried after Diane and Paul to check on her son.

Susan approached with another girl, explaining her friend had invited her to spend the night with her. As soon as Margaret rejoined them and gave her approval, the youngest Peters child rushed away, seemingly unaffected by the night's events.

"Jeff, are you sure about everyone staying with you?" Katie asked once more.

"I'm sure. The only problem I have is there's not much food in the house. I usually eat out. But I'll go shopping in the morning and—"

"Take the food we've got here," Margaret said. "Jack, can you find a sack?"

Jeff started to protest, but Margaret shushed him. "It will go to waste here, and I doubt that Katie needs it. Gabe, can you—"

"Sure, Margaret," Gabe assured her, turning to follow Jack.

They returned quickly with two grocery bags full. Jack put them in the front of Jeff's truck. Gabe added another bag of clothes for Paul.

"There's bacon and eggs and bread, plenty for breakfast, and other stuff," Jack told Jeff.

"Thanks again. I'd better head on out or Paul and Diane will get there ahead of me." He shook Gabe and Jack's hands and nodded to the two ladies. Then he got in and backed out onto the road. Diane had already left, her brother beside her in her car.

When he reached his house, Diane and Paul were waiting in her car. He took his medical bag and unlocked the front door, ushering them in. "We'll have to make up the beds," he muttered. He really wasn't much of a housekeeper. Once a week a lady came in to clean, so it shouldn't be too bad, but he wasn't used to guests. "I'll be right back. I have to bring in the food your mom sent with us so you wouldn't starve."

Diane had made Paul sit down at the table. After patting his shoulder, she came after Jeff. "I'll help."

"I can get them," he assured her, but she ignored him and took one of the bags away from him.

Once inside, she said, "I'll put these away if you'll find the linens for Paul's bed."

He knew she'd already had a long day, but she was emptying the two bags as she spoke. Paul gave him a ragged smile, as if recognizing his confusion. The boy needed to be in bed. With a pain pill, Jeff decided, as he noted the paleness of his face.

Jeff hurried upstairs to locate clean sheets. One bedroom had a king-size bed, like his own. Since he was six foot and Paul already topped him by an inch or two, he chose that bed for the boy. Before he'd gotten half the sheet on, Diane joined him and quickly pulled the other half into place.

"Aren't you exhausted?" he asked, staring at her.

"I'm fine. Where's the top sheet?"

He spread it out and Diane tucked in the corners.

"The pillow cases?"

He gave her one and took the other.

"If you'll find a lightweight blanket, I'll go down and get Paul."

Jeff stood there, his hands on his hips as he watched her leave the room. He felt like saluting. Then he shrugged his shoulders. She was doing what had to be done. He shouldn't complain.

He was spreading out the blanket when Paul and Diane returned. After pulling down the covers, he turned to help them.

Paul's cheeks flushed, which alarmed him. Was he feverish? "Are you hot, Paul?"

"No, but—but I need to, uh, use the facilities," the boy said awkwardly.

"Oh, I should've thought of that," Diane exclaimed. "Come on, I'll—"

"Sis!" Paul protested.

"What?" she asked, staring at him.

"As efficient as you are, Diane, I think Paul can manage on his own," Jeff said quietly.

"I'm his sister!" she snapped. "I'm afraid he'll pass out."

"Di, please," Paul begged.

"Oh, all right!" she said with a huff.

"Gabe put some of your things in my car," Jeff added. "Go ahead to the bathroom while I run get them. I'll find you some clean underwear and a T-shirt to wear to bed."

Paul nodded, stealing a look at his sister.

Jeff looked, too, knowing Paul's reluctance to let his sister help him had upset Diane.

She stared at both of them, her expression grim. Then she bent over to finish tugging the blanket into place.

"Where's the bath?" Paul asked over his shoulder.

"Next door to the right," Jeff said. Then he hurried downstairs.

When Paul was in bed, having swallowed the pain pill with no argument, Jeff and Diane left his room.

"If you'll show me where the rest of the linen is, I'll make my bed," she said.

"I'll help," Jeff insisted. He could see the lines of weariness in her pale face.

"No! I don't need you to take care of me. It's enough that you've taken us in and doctored Paul."

He recognized her stubborn pride and gave in to its demand. Opening the hall closet, he took out the sheets and a blanket and then escorted her to his third bedroom. It was smaller and had a full-size bed, a dresser and one bedside table. A bare room.

"Sorry it's not very—" He shrugged his shoulders, unable to come up with a word to describe the room.

"I'll be fine. Thank you."

"If you need anything, let me know."

"I won't need anything."

She shut the door, managing a small smile before it closed completely.

He stood there, thinking about Diane Peters. She

appeared to be a woman in control, like his wife. Only Jeff's wife had given all her time to her work, leaving little time or attention for their marriage. Is that how Diane would be—if she ever married?

He spun on his heel and strode to his bedroom. He needed to put Diane Peters out of his head. Her tired hazel eyes, her sagging shoulders, her mussed dress that so faithfully followed her trim figure, the blond hair that added to her beauty drew Jeff, but she was going to be a career woman.

The last thing he needed.

JEFF WASN'T SURPRISED when he awoke later than usual around eight the next morning—he'd gotten up several times to check on Paul. What awakened him, however, *was* a surprise. The scent of fresh coffee and crisp bacon wafted up the stairs. Half awake, he imagined a picture-perfect breakfast scene, a lovely blonde standing by the stove, a dainty white apron tied around her waist. The table was set, a small vase of flowers in the center, orange juice at every plate.

In his half dream, the woman turned around and he was staring at Diane Peters. Immediately, he came fully awake, lunging upright, his eyes popping open. What was he thinking?

Chapter Four

"Good morning," Diane said, seeing Jeff enter the kitchen. He looked a bit startled at finding her in front of the stove. "I hope you don't mind that I started breakfast. I was hungry and I expect Paul to be up soon."

"Of course not," he muttered, not quite looking her in the eye.

"If you want to sit down, I can pour you a cup of coffee. The eggs will be ready in a minute."

"I can pour the coffee for both of us," he said, reaching for the cabinet that held the mugs. "And I'm delighted you started breakfast. I haven't had such a nice treat in years."

Diane brought the plate of scrambled eggs to the table and sat down. Jeff's statement that he hadn't had breakfast prepared for him in years had startled her.

Around their house, no one left without some sort of morning meal. After eighteen years of a good breakfast, Diane had continued to eat breakfast through her college years. A good thing, too, since she put in long days.

Jeff seemed to be enjoying his food. He looked up and caught her watching. ''I had no idea you could cook. I thought you were a lawyer.''

''I am a lawyer…or will be when I pass the bar. But that doesn't mean I don't eat.''

''I eat, too, but it's usually at a restaurant…or at your sister's shop. Her sausage rolls are good.''

''Yes, they are.''

A knock on the door startled them. Before Diane could move, Jeff jumped up from his chair. ''That's probably for me. Go ahead and eat.''

She supposed he was used to being on call, but it seemed strange that someone would come to his house rather than use the phone. When Diane turned she saw Katie enter the door, carrying a pan.

''Your sister brought some of those sausage rolls we were just talking about,'' Jeff explained, grinning as he followed Katie into the kitchen. ''I guess she didn't know you could cook, either.''

''I thought I'd save you the trouble,'' Katie said, bending down to kiss Diane's cheek. ''How's Paul this morning?''

''He's still asleep,'' Diane said. ''He took a pain pill last night.''

''He did? He must've really been hurting.'' Katie looked at Jeff. ''You said it was minor.''

Jeff pulled out a chair for Katie and gestured for her to sit while he poured her a cup of coffee and brought it to the table. Then he resettled in his chair.

"A burn is a shock to the body. While he'll recover, it will take a while. I don't want him doing much with that arm."

"Poor Paul. He has a lot of plans for the summer. He needs to stay in shape. Can he exercise?" Katie asked.

Jeff shook his head. "Not at once."

"So he'll have to rest a lot?" Diane asked, wondering how he would do that when they didn't even have a place to live. She started making a mental list of people they might call.

"A few days," Jeff said.

Katie was ahead of Diane. "We'll have to find somewhere for the two of you to stay. Will you be able to take care of him, Diane? You don't have much planned except studying for the next few weeks, do you? Mom will worry about—"

Katie's words reminded Diane of her decision yesterday. "The children!" she said, interrupting her sister's question.

She could tell from the expression on Jeff's face that he realized her problem, too.

"What children?" Katie asked.

"I was going to take care of the two children from the wreck while their mother recovers. Now I don't have anywhere to care for them. How long before the house is livable?"

"I don't know," Katie confessed. "We were trying to convince Mom and Jack to rebuild instead of fixing it. The wiring is outdated and dangerous—obviously. We don't want to go through that again."

"No, of course not," Diane agreed, but she was worried. If they decided to rebuild, she would have nowhere to live all summer. "I'll start looking for something to rent."

Jeff's quiet voice interrupted her panic. "Until you find somewhere, you can bring the children here. While you're watching Paul, you can watch them, too."

Diane was stunned by his generosity and started to say something.

Jeff assured them both that it wouldn't be a problem for him. "I'm not here that much. It will be nice to have company, especially company who cooks like Diane."

"It was only breakfast," she protested, embarrassed by his excessive praise.

"Are you sure, Jeff, because we can ask around. Some of the older people in town have empty rooms. We could pay them some rent and—" Katie began.

"I won't hear of it. Besides, it will save me time by housing two of my patients. I can check the boy and Paul before I go to the office."

Katie seemed satisfied with Jeff's explanation, but Diane wasn't. The man made her too...nervous. She didn't want to spend half her summer in his house. When Katie asked to see Paul before she left, Diane offered to show her to his room while Jeff finished breakfast.

On the stairs, Diane whispered to her sister, "See

if you can find a place for us, Katie. I don't feel right staying here.''

"You don't like Jeff?" Katie asked in surprise.

"He's fine, but—he's used to living alone. I don't think he'll enjoy having a full house.''

"I think he'll like it," Katie said, a smile on her lips. "I've been wondering what we could do for him. He seems lonely to me."

"Katie Dawson! What are you thinking?" Diane demanded, suspicion filling her.

"Why, absolutely nothing, sis. I'm just trying to be sure everyone's covered. I'll ask Mabel or Florence if they have room for you, okay?"

Her promise didn't exactly satisfy Diane. Mabel Baxter and Florence Greenfield, mother of Cal Baxter and wife of George Greenfield respectively, were known for their matchmaking. In fact, it was Florence's bet with her friends that resulted in their sons marrying. Doc, as George Greenfield was known, had enthusiastically fallen into the trap and married Florence, too. And then there was Tuck and Spence, their friends, who'd also fallen prey to the bet.

Since then, Cactus had become a hotbed of marriages. Marriage was fine for others, but Diane had no intention of losing her independence now that she was going to finally be earning a salary that would allow her to travel.

"Katie, you tell them no matchmaking. Do you hear me?"

"I certainly do." She opened the door Diane had stopped in front of and hurried to Paul's bedside.

"Paul, how are you?" she asked gently.

At that moment he rolled onto his injured arm and the pain was visible on his face. "Damn!" he muttered, then immediately apologized. "I didn't know it would hurt this much," he said with a gasp.

"I'll go bring you some breakfast," Diane assured him as she left the room.

Jeff was still sitting at the table, sipping his coffee when she entered.

"How's he doing?" he said.

"He's in a lot of pain. Can he take another pain pill?"

"Of course. Do you have the second one from last night?" Jeff asked, getting to his feet.

"Yes. I'm taking him some breakfast. Do you have a tray?"

He found one for her. "Don't give him coffee. I think there's some orange juice. Try that. I'll go up and check on him."

She dished up the scrambled eggs, along with a few sausage rolls and the last of the bacon. Then she poured a glass of juice. After adding napkins and the pain pill she'd left in the kitchen last night, she carried the tray up the stairs.

"But I don't want another pill," Paul was protesting as she entered, even though his facial expression told her he was still in pain.

Jeff, who was sitting on the edge of the bed, responded, "If you like to suffer, that's fine, but it won't help you get well faster."

"What do you mean?"

"The pills help your muscles relax, which means you heal faster. I don't pass out medicine unless there's a need, Paul. You're not going to be too active for a few days, but if you follow orders, you might be able to start sooner."

Paul's unhappy expression didn't change.

"Maybe some breakfast will sweeten him up," Diane said with a smile for her brother. "Katie brought over some sausage rolls."

"Thanks, sis," Paul said, nodding to Katie who was standing beside the bed. But he also tried to pull his weight to a sitting position and moaned in pain. Jeff immediately supported him while Katie put pillows behind his back.

"Okay, okay, I'll take the pill," Paul said.

"Good for you," Jeff replied.

Paul picked up a sausage roll and began eating.

"Hey, if you don't want all that bacon, I'll take another piece," Jeff said. Paul nodded his head with a grin, which made Diane feel better.

"Thanks," Jeff said as he helped himself to another strip of bacon. "Now, I'd better hit the shower. I need to check on the lady from yesterday's wreck, and see if the children can be released." He looked at Katie. "Can you stay with Paul while Diane goes to pick them up?"

"Yes, of course. Diane, I brought you a few clothes if you want to change. Since I had the baby, there's a lot I can't wear."

"Thanks, Katie. I forgot about clothes last night," Diane said. She'd slept in her underwear the night before, not wanting to ask the doctor for a T-shirt. She figured she'd pick up a big T-shirt at the one discount store in Cactus. She had a little money left over from her last semester in school. Not enough for an entire wardrobe, but she'd manage.

Jeff followed her out of the room and said, ''I didn't think about you having nothing, Diane. I would've offered you some—well, at least a T-shirt. I'm sorry.''

''Don't worry about it. I'm not your responsibility,'' she assured him as she hurried away. The thought of wearing his clothes was doing strange things to her breathing.

JEFF WATCHED HER rush away, as if he carried a disease. She didn't seem to like him much. When he'd seen her in her dress from yesterday, he'd intended to apologize and offer her anything he had. But breakfast—and his dream—had distracted him.

With good reason.

He hurried to the shower. He was anxious to see how his surgery patient was doing. Samantha had probably already checked her, but he would drop by her room before he reassured the children.

It was going to seem strange with children in the house. He'd always wanted kids, but his wife said she had too many children in her life as it was since she was a school counselor.

Maybe he'd find out he didn't want kids after all. That would be good. It would erase some of the regret he felt.

After he'd showered and shaved, he dressed in fresh jeans and a knit shirt. It was wrinkled because he hadn't gotten it out of the dryer in time, but he hoped no one would notice with his white coat on top.

Of course, his white coat was at the office.

It wouldn't be the first time. His nurses always tsked at his appearance, but he ignored them. He wasn't there for a beauty contest.

He went back to Paul's room when he was ready to find Diane in a snug pair of jeans and a T-shirt, her blond hair pulled back in a ponytail. He thought she looked about ten years old...except for her body. All woman.

"Are you ready, Jeff?" Katie asked, distracting him from staring at Diane.

"Uh, yeah. How about you, Diane?"

"Yes." She told her brother and sister goodbye and hurried out of the room in front of him. Which gave him an excellent view of her backside. Definitely all woman.

At the bottom of the stairs, she paused and asked, "May I move the child seat to my car?"

"Sure, if you think there's room," he agreed with a frown. "I suppose I could run you back here."

"No, I'll drive us. I may bring Toby back here and let he and Paul watch each other while I take Janie with me and do a little shopping. Will that be okay?"

"Probably. They can call me if there's a problem."

"No, I'll leave my cell phone number with them."

"Okay. If it needs charging, you can use my charger while you're settling them in."

"Oh, thanks."

He decided they needed to get away from each other before they got so polite they couldn't communicate at all. "I'll see you at the clinic."

Since it was only two blocks from his house, they wouldn't have much of a break. At least he might have enough time to concentrate his attention on his patients rather than Diane's body.

WHEN DIANE GOT TO the room where the two children had spent the night, she discovered a nurse trying to feed Janie while Toby struggled with his left hand.

Janie wasn't cooperating.

When she saw Diane, the little girl almost leaped out of the nurse's hold toward her, her little arms stretched out.

"Well," the nurse said with a sigh, "finally we've found something she likes. You."

Diane lifted the little girl from the nurse's arms and soothed her. Her gaze went to Toby's face and she saw loneliness and fear in his gaze. "Good morning, Toby. How are you?"

"Fine," he mumbled, but his eyes were filling with tears.

"You didn't think I'd forgotten you, did you?"

He shook his head, but he didn't look confident.

The nurse surrendered her chair to Diane and picked up Toby's spoon. "Let me help you finish your breakfast, Toby. You're doing a really good job, but this way you can eat it before it gets cold."

"And I'll tell you why I'm a little late," Diane added. "You won't believe what happened."

"What?" Toby asked, and the nurse slipped in a bite while his mouth was open.

Diane turned the fire into an adventure instead of the disaster it had been. "So we can't stay with my Mom."

"Cookie?" Janie asked.

"What a smart little girl you are to remember about my mama's cookies. But I can make cookies, too. *If* you eat your breakfast."

"So we can't stay with you?" Toby asked, his voice wavering.

"Of course you can, but not at my mother's house. So, for a day or two, we're going to stay with the doctor. Do you remember him? He's taking care of your mother."

"We haven't seen her."

The longing in Toby's voice brought tears to Diane's eyes and she fought to keep them from falling. With a smile, she said, "When Dr. Jeff comes, we'll ask him about her, okay? But he's a good doctor. I'm sure he's taking good care of her."

"I appreciate that vote of confidence," Jeff Hausen said from the doorway.

"The kids are worried—" she started, embarrassed.

"Yeah. Hi, Toby, remember me?"

The boy sort of nodded, but Diane saw the questions in his eyes.

"I just checked on your mom, and she's still sleeping. If she were awake, I'd take you to see her, but she needs her rest. Do you mind waiting until later to see her?"

Diane's heart swelled with pride as the boy bravely shook his head no. He was trying so hard to be the man in the family.

"Nurse, I'll finish feeding Toby his breakfast," Jeff said and soon took the nurse's place. He and the boy had a rambling conversation, covering such topics as pets, favorite foods and friends.

Janie had settled down and was eating some breakfast now that Diane was holding her. "All done?" she asked the little girl when she refused the next bite. "I'd like you to drink your milk all gone, Janie. Okay?" She held the glass to the child's lips and she covered Diane's hands with her own pudgy ones and drank the last drop of milk.

"Good girl!" Diane bragged.

"You, too," Jeff said. "She's apparently been giving everyone a hard time since she got up."

"She's scared." Diane was glad she could help, but she knew Janie's attachment to her was because she'd been the first to arrive at the accident.

"Well, how about I let you two leave the clinic today? You can come back and see your mom whenever you want because my house is only two blocks away."

"When?" Toby asked, his voice anxious.

"As soon as she wakes up, honey," Diane answered.

"Will you call us?" Toby asked, looking at Jeff.

"You bet."

Since the children didn't have anything but the clothes they'd worn yesterday, it didn't take long to pack. As they gathered everything up, she told the two of them about her brother Paul and his hurt arm. She explained that they could help her take care of Paul.

Janie paid her words no attention, clinging to Diane, seeming to fear she would be left behind if she didn't hold on.

Toby seemed to be doing better. When Jeff rolled in the wheelchair, he perked up at the idea of a ride.

But by the time they got to Jeff's house, Toby was exhausted. Even Janie seemed subdued. Diane wasn't sure she'd get any shopping done today. Besides, Katie had brought her a nightshirt as well as another pair of jeans, a pair of navy shorts and several other T-shirts.

All they'd need now were more groceries.

"Are you sure you'll be all right with all of them? I need to go back for office hours," Jeff asked her, touching her arm.

A shiver ran over her skin. "We'll be fine. I may need to go to the grocery store, but I'll hurry. Otherwise—"

She was interrupted by Katie coming down the stairs. "I've already placed an order for groceries.

With five of you to feed, you're going to be busy, Di.''

''Oh, thanks, Katie. Do I go pick it up?''

''No, they'll deliver, and I'm sending over some cookies for—''

Janie began clapping as she heard her favorite word.

Katie laughed.

''Thanks,'' Diane said again. ''I'm going to have to use them as bribery, I think. She's fixated on you know what.''

''Just save one for me. I've had your sister's you know whats before and I don't want to be left out,'' Jeff said, grinning. ''If you're all right, I'll go now.''

''Yes, of course,'' she assured him, trying not to sound too eager.

With a wave of his hand, Jeff went back out to his car.

''You really don't like him?'' Katie asked, curiosity in her eyes.

''He's a stranger, Katie. I don't know him.''

''For a stranger, he's being very generous. Gabe and I like him a lot.''

''But I thought he tried to date you when he first came here?'' she asked in surprise, knowing her brother-in-law's fierce protectiveness of his wife.

Katie laughed. ''He took me to dinner with Doc and Florence when he was visiting. But he wasn't seriously interested. Even Gabe admits that now.'' With another chuckle, she added, ''But it kept him on his toes for a while.''

"Well, I feel like I'm imposing on Jeff. He doesn't know me or the kids and barely knows Paul."

"Sounds to me he's acting like anyone else in Cactus. You know how everyone pitches in when something goes wrong."

"Which is why you'll find a place for us, right?" Diane asked, hoping to push her sister into action.

"I'll try," she promised before she kissed Diane's cheek and hurried out. "I'll be sure to send the you know whats," she called over her shoulder.

With a sigh, Diane closed the door and trudged back up the stairs, Janie in her arms. They'd put Toby in the bed with Paul. The boy seemed more comfortable there. Diane was sure he was afraid of being alone.

"How are you two doing?" she asked from the door.

"We're fine," Paul said, his voice a little slurred from the pain pill.

"Toby, keep an eye on him. He's taken medicine that makes him sleepy," Diane said, smiling to reassure the little boy.

"Toe!"

Diane stared at Janie. "Does your toe hurt?" she asked in surprise.

"No, that's what she calls me," Toby announced. He held out his arms to his little sister.

For the first time since Diane had gotten to the hospital this morning, Janie wanted down. She let the little girl down and the child toddled to the side of the bed.

"Don't try to lift her," Diane warned both males. A knock on the door distracted her. "Oh, I think those are the groceries Katie ordered so I can make you lunch. I'll be right back. Keep an eye on Janie."

JEFF LEFT HIS OFFICE at five. He'd called his house several times to check on his new "family," and Diane had always assured him they were doing fine.

He was anxious to see for himself. He felt responsible for all of them…and he kind of liked the feeling. For a few days, at least, he had a family.

When he opened the back door of his house, his nose immediately picked up the scent of food. There was no reason Diane would cook for him. He didn't expect her to, of course.

But, man, he'd love a good dinner…with Diane beside him. Too often today his mind had dwelled on Diane, on her beauty. He couldn't ignore it. But he also loved her concern for others…her heart. And he couldn't deny the spark he felt every time he touched her. But he was going to have to watch himself. He and Diane weren't right for each other.

When he reached the kitchen, he discovered Diane working at the sink and Janie sitting at the table.

"That's not safe, Diane!" he called as he rushed to the table, picturing the child falling on her head. To his surprise, Diane didn't move except to turn and stare at him.

Chapter Five

At Jeff's loud exclamation, Diane turned from the sink to see little Janie jump a bit, frightened by his voice.

"It's all right, sweetie. Dr. Hausen didn't intend to frighten you." She reassured the little girl as she moved toward the child. She hugged her and showed her again how to stack the aluminum bowls she'd given her to play with, while she sat in the chair, a dishtowel tying her in place.

"I didn't mean—I didn't realize you'd tied her to the chair. Is that wise?" Jeff asked.

Diane gave him a disgusted look. "I may not know about medicine, but I can assure you I know all about taking care of children."

"Okay, my mistake." He paused, staring at her, then added, "I guess that will come in handy when you have your own kids."

Diane returned to the salad she was making. "I'm not having children." She figured her remark would end the conversation. Most people would assume she couldn't for some reason and be embarrassed to ask anything else.

"Why not?"

She turned to look at him. He'd sat down at the table beside Janie and was helping her stack and unstack her bowls.

"I don't want to," she said succinctly, turning away. He was much too handsome in his rumpled shirt, his brown hair falling over his forehead as he bent toward the child. For the first time, she noticed a few silver strands in his hair. She remembered his teasing about his age.

He looked up, trapping her with his blue gaze. "Then why volunteer to take on Janie and Toby?"

"That's different."

"Why?"

She huffed in exasperation. "Do you always ask why?"

"Yeah. It's how I learn things."

"Well, stop trying to learn things about me. Dinner is ready," she announced abruptly, putting the salad she'd been making on the table. "Will you bring the patients down?"

"What are we having?" he asked as he stood, looking around the kitchen. "I thought I smelled— If salad is all you made, I can go get some burgers or something. That won't be enough for—I mean, Toby and Paul are growing boys."

Diane shook her head at him, a wry smile on her face. "I know about growing boys, you included. There will be plenty of food."

As if he didn't trust her, his gaze circled the kitchen again, coming back to the salad. "Are you sure?"

She ignored him. "Come on, Janie, we need to wash your hands so we can eat." She lifted the little girl and left Jeff standing there.

If he wanted to go buy burgers, let him.

JEFF WENT UPSTAIRS to discover Paul and Toby in the big bed. Toby's head was on Paul's shoulder as he read a book to the little boy.

"How are my two patients today?" he asked.

"Hi, Doc," Paul said in greeting.

Toby smiled shyly.

"Maybe you'd better make it Jeff, Paul. Otherwise, Doc will get his feelings hurt."

Paul grinned. "Okay. Hey, when's dinner? Has Diane fixed anything? We're hungry."

"Um, your sister sent me to bring you two to the table, but…well, all I saw was a salad. You know how ladies are, trying to diet. If that's all she's fixed, don't complain. I'll go out and get us some more food later. Okay?"

Paul stared at him. "All she fixed is salad? That doesn't sound like Diane."

"I don't much like salad," Toby mumbled.

"Come on, Toby, green stuff is good for you. Let's wash up and go down. It's the least we can do. Diane didn't have to fix dinner for us."

Paul didn't move, staring at him. "Why not? I thought she was supposed to take care of us."

"And she is. But a lot of women don't include cooking. She's taking care of your injury."

Shaking his head, Paul slid off the bed and stood. When he seemed to waver, Jeff reached out for him.

"I'm okay. I've stayed down too much today."

"You were supposed to. How about you, Toby? Are you feeling okay?" Jeff squatted down to see the little boy's face.

He shrugged and then grimaced. "How's my mama?"

"She's getting stronger," Jeff assured him.

"Did she wake up?"

"No, son, she didn't. Sometimes, they don't wake up until the pain goes away. It's how they keep from hurting so much. You don't want your mama to hurt, do you?"

Toby shook his head, but his gaze was troubled.

"I told her you and Janie were fine and were waiting for her." Jeff had figured it couldn't hurt. Doctors still weren't sure how much a person in a coma could hear.

"Okay," Toby agreed.

Diane and Janie were in the kitchen when the three males arrived. Jeff stared at the table. The salad was there, as it had been when he'd left, but there was also a big platter of fried chicken, potato salad, and a plate with pickles, carrots, cucumbers and celery.

"Where did all this come from?" he asked, astounded.

Diane raised an eyebrow. "From the refrigerator.

I thought cold fried chicken would be easier for the guys to manage.''

Paul laughed. ''Doc, I mean, Jeff, thought salad was all you'd fixed.''

''I know,'' Diane said, keeping her voice even. She was pouring milk for both children and Paul. Then she looked at Jeff. ''Do you want milk, tea or coffee?''

''Iced tea, please.'' He moved over to the kitchen counter. ''But I can pour it. You, too?''

''Yes, please. Wait, Janie,'' she said, as the little girl began reaching for the chicken, ''We're not ready to start yet.''

''Janie,'' Toby ordered sternly. ''Mama told you to wait 'til we said the prayer.''

Janie puckered up. ''Mama!'' she cried, looking around the room.

Diane seemed to take the child's behavior in stride, sitting down and putting her arm around her.

''I'm sorry, Diane,'' Toby said, his eyes filling with tears.

Jeff decided reinforcements were called for before the great meal was ruined. ''Hey, Toby, which part of the chicken do you like?'' he asked, putting Diane's iced tea by her plate before he sat down.

''Yeah,'' Paul added, trying to help out. ''I hope it's not the drumstick.''

Toby looked from one man to the other, his bottom lip still trembling. ''It is the drumstick,'' he whispered, a fearful look on his face.

''Good thing there's two of them,'' Paul teased.

Toby looked from Paul to his little sister. Then he said, "I don't really want a drumstick. Janie can have mine."

Paul looked stricken and Jeff, sitting beside him, put a hand on his shoulder. "Don't worry, Toby. Paul was teasing. He wants a bigger piece, like the breast."

Toby still looked unsure.

Diane came to the rescue. "Fortunately, this chicken had four legs, so there are four drumsticks."

Toby brightened even as Diane pulled Janie's hands together to say the prayer. Then she looked at Jeff and nodded.

Jeff gave a brief prayer. Then he and Diane began passing the food, helping the young ones serve themselves, and making sure Paul didn't use his burned arm.

When Jeff finally got to eat, he bit into the chicken and closed his eyes. It was fantastic. Crispy crust, tender meat.

"Salad?" Diane asked.

He opened his eyes to find the bowl of salad beside him. Then he realized Toby was watching him. He wanted to assure Diane he'd fill up on chicken and nothing else, but he had to set a good example. Scooping up several spoonfuls for his plate, he added some to Toby's plate, too.

"Of course we want salad, don't we, Toby? It goes well with fried chicken, the greatest fried chicken in the world," he added, nodding at Diane.

She'd been a little frosty since he'd come home, but now she smiled. "I'm glad you like it."

When the meal was over, the adults took the children to the den, and put on a video for them to watch.

When Diane started back to the kitchen, Jeff stopped her. "You watch the video. I'll clean up."

"That's not necessary."

Since his words didn't stop her, he followed her to the kitchen. "Diane, you cooked. It's only fair that I clean up."

"Please, Jeff, it won't take long. I did most of the cleanup earlier."

"All the more reason for you to rest."

"Because you did nothing all day long? I volunteered for this job. I'll do it." She turned her back on him and began loading the dishwasher.

After a lingering look at her backside, in those tight jeans she'd been wearing earlier, he began stacking the dishes and carrying them to the sink.

"Your husband is going to be a lucky man," he said, paying her the ultimate compliment in his mind.

"I'm not marrying," she said calmly as she began rinsing the dishes.

Jeff turned to stone. No husband? No children? What was going on here?

"Why?"

"I was expecting that question. Have you ever heard of choices, doctor?"

"Yeah, but yours seem a little unnatural."

She stiffened and turned around to glare at him. "Don't tell me you're one of those guys who think women should be barefoot, pregnant and in the kitchen."

"No! But you're an expert cook and great with kids. I just thought—"

"My mother taught all of us how to cook. Even the boys. And we're all good with children because there were so many of us. That doesn't mean I want to continue doing the same things for the rest of my life. I'm going to travel and learn about the world. I'm going to dance on moonlit beaches and fly faster than light. I'm going to sail on the ocean and climb mountains. I'm going to—" She stopped abruptly and began loading the dishwasher again.

Jeff stared at her. It seemed there were hidden depths beneath that beautiful blond hair. "So you have the soul of an adventurer?"

She shrugged her shoulders. "I want to make my own choices."

"But you chose to come back to Cactus?" He remembered his question after their meal at The Last Roundup. She hadn't given him much of an answer. Would she now?

"If you'll clean off the table, I'll sweep," she said as she closed the dishwasher. "Then we'll be finished."

"Aren't you going to answer me?"

"No," she said without showing any emotion.

BEFORE THEY COULD join the kids, the doorbell rang. Again Jeff assured her it would be for him and hurried from the room.

But when she heard Cal's voice, she put on a pot of coffee.

She pulled out the tray she'd used that morning for Paul's breakfast and put a plate of cookies on it thinking she'd take it into the den for Paul and the kids. Then she fixed another plate for the kitchen table.

"Aha! Cookies!" Cal said, as the two men entered the kitchen. He turned to Jeff. "The Peters ladies make the best cookies in the world."

"Thanks, Cal. How about some coffee to go with them?"

"You read my mind, Diane. I'd love some."

"You, Jeff?"

"Yeah, Diane, that would be great."

"I'm here to tell you what I found out about the mother and I brought a suitcase filled with the kids' clothes."

"Oh, wonderful. I intended to buy them a few things today, but I didn't leave the house once we got home from the hospital." Then Diane added, "Let me take some of Katie's cookies to the kids first. I'll be right back." She poured some lemonade in three glasses, put them on the tray and slipped from the kitchen.

Jeff watched her go, amazed that after all the dinner she'd fixed, she didn't even appear tired.

"You're one lucky son of a gun," Cal said, catching his attention.

"What do you mean?"

"You've got Diane here to cook for you and she's pretty as all get-out."

It wasn't that Jeff disagreed with what Cal said. In fact, he thought Cal's assessment was understated. But Cal was Mabel's son, the first of the matchmakers' successes. He didn't want anyone to get any ideas.

"She's a good cook, but her being here is only temporary, you know," he said gruffly, avoiding Cal's gaze.

"Too bad. I've thought you seemed a little lonely, sometimes." Cal took a sip of his coffee.

Jeff reached for a cookie and jammed it into his mouth, hoping Cal would think he didn't answer because he was too busy chewing.

Diane came back into the kitchen. "What did you find out, Cal?" she asked as she sat down.

"Ms. Evelyn Duncan is twenty-nine, a widow, with two children, Toby, four, and Janie, two. She works at a grocery store in Lubbock, rents an apartment nearby, and doesn't have much. The place was spotless, everything in order. The kids' clothes are inexpensive and they don't have too much, but they were all freshly laundered."

"I knew she was a good mother," Diane murmured.

"Why do you say that?" Jeff asked. He'd come

to the same conclusion, but he was interested in her reasons.

"The way the children behave. Toby giving up his favorite piece of chicken for his little sister."

"What's that?" Cal asked, frowning.

Jeff shrugged. "Nothing. Diane saved the day by cooking a four-legged chicken."

"Colonel Sanders must be happy about that," Cal teased, looking at Diane.

She smiled at Cal, and Jeff was surprised by a pang that shot through him. He wasn't jealous. Of course not. But Diane seemed more at ease with Cal than with him.

"Anyway, there is no family, like the little guy said. And not much savings to pay for her medical care. She has some basic insurance, but not much else."

"I figured," Jeff said.

"How's she doing?"

"She's still unconscious. We can't do much until the swelling goes down. I'm hoping she'll wake up when that happens. I've contacted a specialist in Lubbock. He's coming out to verify my diagnosis. Her other injuries are healing."

Diane looked at him. "When can the children see her? They're very anxious to do so."

"I know, but I'm afraid all the tubes and wires will upset them," he pointed out.

"We'll explain about all that before they go in. But...I think Toby is afraid she's dead and we're not telling him." She gnawed on her bottom lip.

Jeff stared at her mouth, full and soft, mesmerized

by her action. Then he shook his head and looked away...straight into Cal's knowing stare. There was a grin on the other man's face.

"Uh, well, then, probably tomorrow" Jeff stammered. "Let's wait until the other doctor checks her in the morning. Then I'll call you."

She nodded her head and stared at her hands, folded on the table.

"I've been thinking," Cal said, drawing their attention.

"Yeah?" Jeff urged, hoping Cal's thought would take his mind off Diane.

"Let's put the matchmakers to work, planning a money raiser for Evie."

"Evie?" Diane asked.

"That's what her neighbors called her when I talked to them. She seems like a good woman trying to take the place of her dead husband and struggling. Cactus is full of good people. Let's give them a way to help her and have some fun, too."

"What a great idea!" Diane exclaimed. "We could provide some work for the teens, too, keep them out of trouble."

"Hey, I hadn't even thought of that benefit," Cal said with a grin. "That would give my deputies a break from all the hell-raising that goes on around here in the summer."

Jeff smiled at the two of them. Here was the difference between Houston and a small town. In Houston, everyone would pass the problem on to a government agency because they were all too busy.

Not just Houston, of course. It happened in all big cities. But in Cactus, they tried to solve problems themselves.

"I think that's a great idea, and I'll do anything I can to help."

Cal laughed. "Be careful what you say, Jeff. In this town, that can be dangerous."

"Maybe that's why I like it here," Jeff returned, but his gaze shifted to Diane. Her cheeks were flushed with enthusiasm and she was smiling at Cal. Because of his concentration on her bottom lip, without thinking of the consequences, he said, "I think a kissing booth at a fair would raise a lot of money." He'd spend his last dollar if Diane was the kisser.

Cal's grin got even bigger. "Hey, good idea! We'll set up a fair on the town square. The boys can build booths and paint them. We can sell baked goods. Have a dunking booth, and, as you said, a kissing booth. I've got a set of darts. We can blow up balloons and have contests popping the balloons. Lots of different things."

"I'm sure Katie will donate cookies and things," Diane said.

"Yeah," Cal added, "and Jack will be perfect to supervise the boys. He's good with kids and a hammer."

"Sam and I could set up a booth to give the required shots for school for a dollar donation," Jeff offered. "I know it wouldn't be a lot of fun but—"

Diane smiled at him, the warmest smile she'd

given him since they'd met. "But it would make it easy for the parents and the kids wouldn't protest as much. I think that's a good idea."

"And then you could get in the dunking booth and let them get their revenge," Cal said with a laugh. "This is great. I'll drop by Mom's on the way home and get the ball rolling. Maybe it will give her something to think about besides weddings."

Diane and Jeff both kept silent at the mention of one of the matchmakers.

Still grinning, Cal stood. "I'll be on my way. The suitcase with the kids' things is in the hallway, Diane. I'm sure Mom will contact you tomorrow about the fair."

"Of course, Cal. Do you want some cookies to take home with you?" Diane asked.

Jeff stared at the plate of cookies. He didn't want her to give away the cookies. He hadn't had home-made cookies in a while.

"Thanks, but between Jess and Mom, I eat too many of them as it is. I'd better leave them. I think you have some bottomless pits here."

Jeff stood too, not looking at Diane. "Thanks for coming by, Cal."

"No problem. Glad to hear the kids are doing well."

DIANE SLID INTO THE bed beside a sleeping Janie. The little girl was clutching a floppy stuffed animal she called "Rabby."

Toby had explained it was a rabbit. They seemed pleased to have their own things around them. They both fell asleep easily.

It reminded Diane of sharing a room with her sisters, first Katie and then Raine. She'd been thrilled to have her own bed finally. But there was a sweetness to having Janie close beside her that she hadn't felt in a long time.

She was tired tonight, but it was a satisfying tiredness. She'd made the children happy today, made them feel a little more secure. And she'd cooked a good meal for all of them. She grinned at Jeff's reaction to the thought of salad for dinner. The silly man! As if she thought that would satisfy a man after working all day.

It struck her that all her plans for the future had never produced the satisfaction she felt tonight. She liked cooking; she liked children. She even liked making a man happy. At least she did if that man was Jeff.

A shudder ran through her. Not Jeff! She didn't mean that. It was just that he appreciated what she did. She'd promised herself she wasn't going to be an accessory to a man…like her mother had been…unable to make a move without a man's guidance.

Her satisfaction was because she'd made the decisions…and it was temporary. She'd be back to her plan for her life. In a year, she could be sure that her family didn't need her. The children would be back with their mother. And she'd find that exciting life she wanted.

Thumping her pillow, she turned over. Thinking about satisfying Jeff Hausen wasn't a good idea. The man was handsome, warm, charming, kind to children. Listing his good points wasn't productive either. She had no interest in any man, much less one as settled in a small town as Jeff was.

She was going to lead a different life.

It was about time.

Chapter Six

Edith Hauk drew a deep breath before she said hesitantly, "Are you sure we're doing the right thing?"

The other three ladies came to an abrupt halt. They'd each been making a list of things to be done for the fund-raising fair they'd been planning. Now their pencils were still, their gazes on Edith.

"What are you talking about, Edith?" Mabel Baxter asked.

"You know I'm talking about Diane."

Florence Greenfield, another of the original co-conspirators to bring love, marriage and especially grandchildren to certain people in Cactus, asked, "What have we done?"

"Well, nothing yet, but—"

"Edith Hauk, how can you suggest we're doing something wrong when you enthusiastically did the same thing for Spence?" Ruth Langford asked, staring at her friend. "Aren't you glad Spence found Melanie? Aren't you happy about your grandchildren?"

"Well, yes, of course I am. But he's my son. His happiness is my business."

"I think happiness is everyone's business," Florence said briskly and picked up her pencil. "Besides, we haven't done anything yet."

"We've decided not to open our homes to Diane and those poor children…and Paul, I guess."

Mabel said very slowly, "But we're only doing that because we're trying to raise money for the children's mother. Look at your list. Will you have time for houseguests if you manage to get all that work done?"

"Well, no, but—"

"Isn't it important to help the poor woman?" Ruth asked.

"Of course, but—"

"Doesn't Margaret deserve to have more grandchildren as much as us?" Florence asked.

Before Edith could protest again, Mabel pointed out, "Besides, Diane hasn't asked us to take her in."

"She asked her sister."

Mabel beamed. "Exactly! And Katie agrees with us. Both Diane and Jeff need someone. Poor Diane has concentrated on work and studies for too long. It's time she had some fun."

"Maybe the doctor isn't her idea of fun," Edith timidly offered.

"You don't like Dr. Jeff? He's so handsome, and his bedside manner is so gentle and patient," Ruth chimed in.

"Of course I like him. He's perfect for us here in

Cactus. And I know he seems a little lonesome,''
Edith agreed. ''But what if Diane doesn't interest
him?''

''Dear Edith, we're not going to force anything.
If they aren't interested in each other, then letting
Diane and the others stay at his house won't hurt
anything.''

''That's true,'' Edith agreed, but she was still
frowning.

''So, we'll help this nice lady and her children.
And everyone will think better of Jeff for helping
out. You know, some of our citizens are still ad-
justing to having a new doctor.''

Edith's face brightened. ''You're right. We'll be
making things easier for the doctor. Okay, I'm in,
but I hope Diane calls one of you first.''

JEFF KNEW HE WAS IN trouble when he woke up the
next morning.

He could hear the other shower running. His mind
immediately pictured Diane Peters naked under the
spray of warm water.

So much for lingering in bed. Next he'd imagine
her on the pillow next to his.

What was wrong with him? He didn't want to
answer that question, so he threw back the covers
and headed for his own shower. If there was warm
water left, maybe he could stay in the shower long
enough to wash away those thoughts.

If only cold water was left, all the better.

When he stepped out of the shower, he could

smell the scent of coffee climbing the stairs again. He could get used to a woman in his kitchen, his house, his bed...Whoa! The effect of the cold shower hadn't lasted long.

He'd loved his wife. She'd been a good woman. But she'd been so wrapped up in her work, she hadn't paid much attention to their marriage. His work was absorbing, but he'd wanted a more balanced life—children, love, togetherness.

They'd been married five years and had grown more and more distant to each other. He'd tried to encourage his wife's career, but he'd ended up resenting the fifteen-hour days she put in.

He had to be careful now. Diane was beautiful. A wonderful cook. Terrific with children. All the things a man could want in a wife. But she didn't want that kind of life. She had no intention of joining her life with a man's.

Besides, she was too young for him.

But he could enjoy her cooking for a few days. He could look forward to coming home, to sharing his time with the children, to visiting with Paul. No more long evenings with nothing to occupy his time.

When he entered the kitchen, he discovered Diane in shorts and a T-shirt, standing at the stove, scrambling eggs.

"You really don't have to cook every morning, Diane," he said.

She looked up from the stove, her face clean of makeup, a smile on her lips. "I love breakfast. And the kids will be up shortly, starving to death."

"You think so? Isn't it still a little early for them?"

Diane shook her head. "Most kids I've been around wake up early. It's only when they reach the teenage years that you have to drag them out of bed."

"How about Paul? Will he sleep late?"

"No. He's always been an early riser. Susan, on the other hand," she said, naming her youngest sister, "has to be pulled from bed. And since one of her chores is gathering the eggs, she has to be up early."

"It can't take that long to gather a few eggs," Jeff pointed out as he poured a couple of mugs of coffee, handing one to Diane.

She laughed. "We started out gathering at least four dozen and selling three of them. After Dad died, Katie increased our production to six dozen. And after gathering them, Susan has to wash them and put them in boxes for our customers."

"Before school?" Jeff asked, frowning.

"Definitely. Raine and I were in charge in the beginning. Paul helped Susan until he started college. Now, our only customer is Katie, and we've cut back. But it still has to be done early."

"What happens when Susan goes off to college?"

Before she answered, Diane emptied the scrambled eggs onto a platter already half-filled with bacon. She carried the platter to the table, then went back for her mug Jeff had poured her. "I don't know," she admitted as she sat down.

"I guess nothing stays the same," Jeff commented. He tried to think of another topic of conversation. He'd discovered he enjoyed company at the breakfast table.

"Yes, and I bet you'll be glad when we're out of your hair. I asked Katie to check around for a place for us, but I haven't heard from her. I'll make some calls today."

Jeff's heart lurched. "Uh, I don't think that's necessary. It's not like I need the room. And I'm getting great meals. By the way, I have an account at the grocery store. I'll call them this morning and have your name added to the account."

"No! I'm sure that won't be necessary. It would look like—I mean, we'll be moving out either today or tomorrow."

"What if you can't find anything?"

She didn't look at him. "I'm sure we'll find somewhere to stay."

Jeff stopped trying to persuade her to forget moving out. He didn't want her thinking he wanted them to stay. "Well, if you're still here this evening and cook another meal, put it on my account."

"We'll see," she muttered.

Sounds of movement upstairs had Diane jumping to her feet. "I think that's Janie. I'll go see if the kids are up."

In no time the table was full, all five of them enjoying breakfast. Jeff sat, listening to Janie's plaintive plea for more juice, Toby's conversation with Paul about dogs, and Diane's soothing voice, enjoying himself. Through his lonely childhood, his disastrous teen years, even his married days, he'd wanted the sounds of a family.

"Dr. Jeff, you said I could see—" Toby broke off and stared at his little sister. "I mean, you said I could go with you," he finished, staring at Jeff.

Jeff, too, looked at Janie. She was carrying a spoonful of eggs to her mouth, using both hands.

"Don't take such big bites, Janie," Diane cautioned in a gentle voice.

"Yes, I did, Toby. Let me make a phone call to see if she can receive visitors." Jeff didn't want to promise a visit only to discover the woman had taken a turn for the worse. "Diane, will, uh, the little one be okay?"

Their gazes met and Jeff loved the instant communication. He didn't have to explain his concerns.

"Janie and I are going to the grocery store today," she announced, seemingly unrelated to Jeff's question. "Right, Janie? We're going to bake a cake this afternoon, just us girls."

Janie beamed at Diane, nodding enthusiastically. "Cake!"

"Good. I'll look forward to eating some tonight," Jeff assured the little girl. "How about you, Paul? Do you have anything you need to do today? I'll need to check your bandage before I go."

Paul looked at Toby, then Jeff. "I thought I'd hang out with you and Toby. When he's through with his, uh, visit, we can walk over to The Lemon Drop Shop and have a lemonade."

Jeff knew how difficult the visit would be for Toby. The four-year-old would be frightened by his mother's appearance. He was grateful Paul was willing to help the little boy. "Great idea. Thanks."

When breakfast was over, Diane sent Janie upstairs to dress herself. Paul and Toby followed her.

"Is she old enough to get dressed?" Jeff asked.

"She may not match everything, but it's good for her to try. And it gives me time to clean the kitchen before I help her finish up."

"I'll help."

"Really, that's not necessary."

He ignored her protest and began clearing the table. "I don't have any appointments until nine-thirty." In minutes, they had the kitchen in order.

"Did you tell Paul to go with Toby?" he asked, curious.

"No. But Paul's a sensitive guy, even though he'd die if he heard me say that."

Jeff grinned. "Yeah, most girls go for the macho men instead of the sensitive ones. Is that true of you?"

DIANE THOUGHT MOST girls didn't know what they were doing. Her father had been macho. She'd loved him, but when he'd died, she'd discovered some problems. Her father had protected her mother to such a point, she didn't know how to handle life.

It was Katie who'd saved the family. Not a macho guy.

"No, not really. But then, I'm not interested in

either kind.'' She headed for the door, preferring not to discuss her taste in men. She was finding her host too attractive for her to feel comfortable.

''Diane!'' he called, stopping her.

She looked over her shoulder, keeping her distance. ''Yes?''

''Charge the groceries to me.''

''I told you—''

''My house, my groceries. If you don't, I won't be able to eat anything. And I've got my heart set on a piece of that cake.''

''You're being unreasonable,'' she returned, irritated by his order.

''Well, one of us is,'' he said with a grin that made his blue eyes sparkle.

''Fine! I'll charge it to your account, but it's going to be a very costly cake!'' she snapped.

''I can afford it,'' he assured her, still grinning.

Men! They always had to win.

She stomped out of the kitchen.

JEFF KEPT TOBY BETWEEN him and Paul as they walked down the hall to see the little boy's mother. The specialist had confirmed his diagnosis. Evie would regain consciousness when the swelling went down. ''You understand your mom will still be asleep, Toby?''

The child nodded, his bottom lip trembling as he looked up at Jeff. ''But she's gonna be all right?''

''I hope so,'' Jeff replied, unable to lie to the boy. At this stage, he couldn't promise a complete recovery. He lifted his eyes to see Paul staring at him approvingly.

"Hey, Tobe," Paul chimed in, "you've got the best doctor for your mom. She's lucky to have Jeff take care of her."

Toby nodded again.

When they reached the closed door, Jeff swung the little boy into his arms. Then he pushed open the door and stood there, not moving, giving Toby time to take in the sight of his mother.

Paul rubbed Toby's back as the boy gulped back tears.

"I'm going to take you to her bedside now, Toby," Jeff said softly. "If you talk to her, I think she may be able to hear you. I want you to hold her hand and tell her you and Janie are fine, and that you want her to get well, so you can be together. Okay?"

Toby nodded again.

Jeff pulled up a chair by the bed and sat down, putting Toby in his lap.

"Mama?" Toby said, but his voice wavered. Jeff gave him a hug.

The little boy gingerly reached out to hold her hand. Then he said, "Mama, me and Janie are fine. I'm taking care of her. Diane and Dr. Jeff and Paul are helping us, but we miss you." Toby gulped back tears. "Get well, Mama." Then he turned and buried his face in Jeff's shirt.

Jeff had been watching the woman's reaction, and he noted an increase in her pulse rate. He leaned toward Paul and whispered, "Take Toby out in the hall."

After the pair had departed, Jeff watched the woman's vital signs, but he saw no other change. With a sigh, he joined the others.

"Nice job, Toby. I promise you she's getting better."

"Did she wake up?"

"Not yet. But I think she will soon. Especially if you come visit every day." Jeff looked at Paul. "Thanks for coming with Toby." He pulled his wallet from his jeans and took out a ten. "You two go have some cookies and lemonade, okay?"

Paul stared at the money. "I don't pay at my sister's shop, Jeff."

"I do. Take the money," Jeff ordered with a grin. "Toby needs to have a little fun."

Paul reluctantly took the money. "You were real good with him, Jeff. You'll make a good dad some day."

"So will you, Paul. Thanks for helping out."

He stood there in the hallway, watching the two disappear. He'd intended to have children one day. He'd wanted to be the dad he hadn't had. But it hadn't happened. Maybe Paul would have kids. It seemed to be catching in Cactus.

JANIE AND DIANE FINISHED the grocery shopping by filling the basket to the top. Feeding five people required a fair amount of food. She'd realized it would take several days to find a place, probably. As soon as she got back to the house, she was going to call Katie and see if she'd checked with anyone.

In the meantime, they were going to eat well. It wasn't that she spent a lot to punish Jeff for being so insistent. Well, maybe a little, but the man had had practically nothing in his house when they'd first arrived. Didn't he know about eating healthy?

At least when she left, he'd have a stock of food for a few days.

"Please put these groceries on Dr. Hausen's account," she said to the checker, hoping he'd remembered to call.

"Dr. Hausen?" the woman repeated, staring at Diane. Then she said, "Oh, you're Katie's sister, aren't you? I came to town after you went off to school. These are for the doc? He's a handsome man. You two an item?"

Diane drew a deep breath. Small-town gossip. "No, we're not. He said he'd call and—"

"Betty Sue?" the woman shouted, which, of course, drew more attention.

"Yeah, hon?" the store manager called back.

"Did that handsome young doctor call about buying groceries for Katie's sister?"

Diane felt her cheeks turn bright red. How ridiculous! She felt like a kept woman.

"I'm doing the cooking there," she said, hoping people wouldn't start rumors that were a lot more exciting than the truth.

"You're his housekeeper? I thought you were

gonna be a lawyer. Well, don't worry, dear. I'm sure you'll make it eventually.''

"I am a lawyer!" Diane snapped, then added, more sedately, "as soon as I pass the bar.''

"Well, good for you," the checker said with a big smile.

Betty Sue interrupted them, breathless from rushing over. "Sorry I forgot to tell you he called. Hi, Diane. Dr. Jeff said all your purchases should be added to his bill. Are you and he, you know, *good friends?*''

"I'm taking care of my brother and the children from the wreck, and Dr. Hausen is letting us stay at his house. I'm doing the cooking. That's all. I only met him two days ago. There's nothing going on!" she finished, her voice rising with each word.

Both women stared at her. "Didn't mean to pry," the checker muttered.

"I don't know what you're getting so upset about," Betty Sue added. "He's the catch of the town. Every lady from eighteen to fifty has been visiting him with all kinds of strange ailments. He don't even notice.''

"Yeah, you're lucky he's looking at you.''

Diane closed her eyes. Where was her patience? "I'm sorry, but there's nothing going on.''

The checker began filling bags. "Okay, if you say so.''

"Oh, I do.''

As soon as she got Janie in the car seat and the groceries in her little car, she hurried back to the doctor's house, waiting until a car passed before she got out.

How silly of her. Everyone probably knew by now that she and Paul and the children were staying *temporarily* at the doctor's. As soon as she got inside, she'd make sure it ended soon.

She put the groceries away, found something to occupy Janie, and dialed Katie's number.

Her mother answered.

"Mom, is Katie there?"

"No, she's at the shop. Do you need something?"

"I asked her to look around for somewhere else for us to stay. I thought maybe—"

"Why would you move somewhere else? Isn't the doctor being nice? I liked him. I'm sure you must've—"

"Mom! This was temporary. Never mind. I'll go see Katie at the shop. Talk to you later." She'd known better than to talk to her mother. She loved her, but Kate was the one who accomplished things.

"Janie, want another ride in the car?" she asked, breathing deeply, trying to stay calm.

"Car!" Janie exclaimed and came running.

She loaded her back in the car seat and drove the four blocks to her sister's shop. She parked the car before she saw Paul and Toby sitting at one of the outside tables. She led Janie over to them. "How did it go?"

Paul said, "Really well. Toby was great."

"Toe!" Janie called and hugged her big brother.

"Can Janie have a cookie?" Toby asked.

"Of course. In fact, I need to talk to Katie, Paul. Can you keep an eye on both of them?"

Paul agreed and Diane slipped inside the shop. It was crowded, as usual.

"Why, Diane, I haven't seen you since you got back," one lady said when Diane entered. "I hear you and the new doctor are an item. Congratulations!"

Chapter Seven

Jeff opened the door of his house that afternoon and took in the sounds and smells that signified home to him. It changed the walls of his house into a home.

He smiled and moved quietly inside. When he pushed open the door to the kitchen, he couldn't hold back his pleasure. "Hi, honey, I'm home."

He laughed as he said those words, somehow believing Diane would understand his little joke.

That belief disappeared when a loaf of bread flew through the air and plopped against his face. In the sudden silence, he looked up from the bread he'd caught to see Diane rush past him up the stairs.

"What's wrong?" he asked, frowning.

Paul, who'd been staring after his sister, said, "I don't know. She's been edgy ever since we got home."

Janie whimpered and Toby's eyes were wide with worry.

Paul reluctantly stood. "I guess I'd better go—"

"No," Jeff said, "I caused the problem. I'll go straighten things out. Keep the kids here."

Jeff put down his medical bag and some papers. Then he left the kitchen, taking the stairs two at a time.

After knocking on the bedroom door, with no response, he opened it to discover Diane lying across the bed, her face covered.

"Diane?"

She didn't answer, so he took several steps into the room.

That action got a response.

"Go away!"

"I didn't mean to upset you. I was teasing," he said softly, ignoring her inhospitable words.

She raised up on the bed and glared at him. There were no tears, as he'd feared, but she was angry. "Do you know what everyone in town is saying? Do you realize—of course you don't. You're not used to a small town."

"What? What are they saying?"

"They think we're—we're sleeping together. They think I'm trying to catch you. Everyone in the grocery store thinks I'm a kept woman!"

Which explained her reaction to his teasing. "Ah. I guess my words weren't too funny, huh?"

"Oh, they were hysterical!" she snapped.

"My idea to pay for the groceries wasn't too discreet either. It didn't occur to me that—"

"You've been here a year, Hausen. Get a clue!

Everything you say and do is fodder for the gossips. That's what a small town is all about.''

He sat down on the edge of the bed. ''Okay, so I didn't think. But it's not such a tragedy, is it? I mean, we're both adults, single. If people want to think we're—'' He broke off, unable to even talk about sleeping with Diane without responding to the thought. He cleared his throat. ''We're not breaking any laws.''

''If we were moving out right away, I wouldn't think much about it. We could avoid each other and the talk would go away,'' Diane explained, sitting up. ''But I can't find anywhere to go.''

Relief filled him. He didn't want them to go away. ''You can't?'' he asked, trying to sound concerned.

''I couldn't believe it. All the people I called said they'd be glad to take us in after the festival they're planning to help Mrs. Duncan.''

''Hey, a few more days won't be a problem,'' Jeff assured her.

''A few more days? They've scheduled the festival for the fourth of July! They think they'll make more money then because everyone comes in town for the Fourth of July celebration.''

''Sounds like good planning.''

She grabbed his arms and shook him, exasperation on her face. ''Don't you get it? That means we have to stay here another month! Today is the seventh of June. By that time, the town will be expecting wedding bells!''

Clearing his throat he said, ''Well, I'm sure they

won't say things to embarrass us. They'll understand. After all, Paul is here.''

''Every time we go out in public, everyone will whisper behind our backs!''

''But you're planning on leaving town, eventually. You said so. If anyone is upset, it should be me,'' he pointed out. ''So don't worry about it.''

''I have to stay for a year. I promised Gabe and Mac and Alex. I wanted to be sure Susan was okay and wouldn't cause any problems for Katie.''

Jeff patted her shoulder. ''You know how quickly the gossips find someone else to talk about. We'll be careful in public. If we keep our distance, they'll forget about us in no time.''

She gave a big sigh. ''I suppose so.'' After a second she looked up. ''I'm sorry about the bread. I was so upset, and then you sounded so—so—happy!''

''I am happy. I'm getting great meals. My house isn't lonely anymore. I'm pleased.''

''Why haven't you remarried if that's the way you feel?'' she asked, a puzzled look on her face.

''I don't know. After my wife died—''

''Oh, of course. It's probably too soon. But I'll help you. I'll look for someone for you to marry. Obviously, you like kids. Maybe the children's mother would be right for you. She's a widow and—''

Jeff was upset and he didn't know why. ''Damn it, does everyone in this town have a matchmaker gene? Can't you accept a single person without trying to match them up with someone?''

''I just thought—'' Diane stared at him, surprise on her face. ''I'm sorry. You're right. I was being presumptuous. But you seemed to like the idea of— I won't play matchmaker, I promise.''

''Good. We'll keep our distances in public and everything will be okay. Now, how about we go downstairs? The kids are worried.''

''Oh, the poor babies. I bet I scared them. You'd better come down with me or they'll think I've scarred you for life.'' Diane jumped up from the bed and started to the door. When she realized he hadn't moved, she stopped. ''Aren't you coming?''

''Yeah, I'm coming,'' he agreed and stood to follow her back to the kitchen.

THE NEXT SEVERAL DAYS were calm. Diane did a lot of cooking, and she took care of the children. Paul began jogging every morning to get back in shape. Jeff kept his enthusiasm for his houseguests to himself.

They were all at the breakfast table Friday morning when Jeff told Paul he could begin doing a little more. ''Just take it easy. No longer than an hour the first day. You might try some tennis. It would be good for your arm.''

''I don't have anyone to play with,'' Paul muttered. ''My friends are out of town.''

''Maybe after I get home tonight we could play. The courts are lighted, aren't they?''

The high school had nice courts. "Hey, would you mind?" Paul asked, his eyes lighting up.

"No, I'd enjoy it," Jeff said. "Do you mind, Diane? It will leave you alone with the kids."

"Of course not, but if you're going to play for an hour, I might take the kids along and let them play at the nearby playground."

"Good idea. Janie, want to go swing tonight?" Jeff asked, smiling at the little girl. He and Toby were becoming friends, but Janie still clung to Diane.

She beamed at him and clapped her hands. "I wuv to swing!"

"All right," Jeff agreed, smiling back.

"In fact," Diane said, "I could make a picnic dinner. Unless you don't want cold fried chicken again so soon."

Jeff laughed. "If anyone votes against the fried chicken, they're out of the family!"

The two children giggled and Paul laughed.

"I think that might be good," Jeff agreed after the laughter subsided. "We could play for a while, then rest Paul's arm. It's amazing how quickly the body loses strength. After eating, we could play a little more."

Paul agreed with that assessment. "If I play all three days, by Monday, maybe I can get back to my regular workouts...after I beat you."

Diane relaxed more than she had in several days. "Paul's a fierce competitor. He doesn't like to be beaten."

"Me, neither," Jeff assured her with a grin. "But from what I've heard, tonight may be my only chance to get him while he's down."

"That's right," Paul agreed. "I'm coming back fast."

When they finished breakfast and the children were upstairs dressing, Jeff asked, "Are you sure it's not too much trouble, fixing a picnic dinner?"

"No, of course not. And it will vary the routine a little for the kids. They'll enjoy playing. There might even be some other children there."

"I guess they've been pretty isolated," Jeff said. "It didn't even occur to me that they'd need more…entertainment."

"You've had a lot to think about. How is their mother?"

"I think she's doing better. Toby's visits are doing her some good. I really have a feeling it won't be much longer before she wakes up."

"Really?" Diane said, her voice rising in excitement.

"Yeah, but she won't be out of the hospital for several weeks afterward. Do you need to be studying or working for the law firm?"

"I've been studying after Janie goes to sleep at night. Or sometimes when she naps. But Gabe called today. He's got a case for which he needs some research done. I told him I'd try to start Monday, spending a few hours there."

"How will you manage?"

"Mom said she'd come over and watch the kids," Diane said. "It won't be a problem."

With a grin, Jeff said, "That's one of the advantages of a small town."

"I guess so."

The kitchen was clean and Jeff leaned down to kiss her on her cheek in thanks for working things out, he guessed. It seemed a natural thing to do. Only she turned her head to ask him something and his lips landed smack on hers.

The surprise had him pulling back. But his body didn't like that response. His lips returned to hers without his input. Or at least that's what he told himself. His arms joined in, wrapping themselves around her and pulling her tightly against him.

When she resisted, and she finally did, he released her at once. "Uh, sorry!" he exclaimed. His voice was hoarse and his breathing rapid. "I was going to—to kiss your cheek. To thank you. I didn't intend—"

While he was stuttering his explanation, Diane was backing away to the kitchen cabinet, staring at him as if he were the devil himself.

"Come on, Diane, it wasn't that big a deal," he said, taking a few steps in her direction. "I'm sure you've been kissed before."

She stuck her hand out, clearly a stop sign, and he halted.

"Say something!" he finally exclaimed.

"Go to work," she ground out. She didn't seem to want to discuss their encounter.

What could he do? He picked up his medical bag and walked out of the kitchen, trying to ignore his body's protest.

DIANE DREW IN DEEP gulps of air. Of course she'd been kissed before! But never like that. Why? That was the question that bothered her. She knew he hadn't planned to kiss her. The first kiss was awkward, accidental. It was the second kiss that made her knees weak.

She wasn't even a virgin. She'd slept with a boyfriend in college. She'd thought he was the one. That they'd have a wonderful life together. Until he told her there was no point in her going to college any longer. She'd be staying at home having the babies while *he* had a career.

She'd dumped him at once.

And hadn't missed him. She sure hadn't missed the sex. She wasn't sure why some women thought it was important at all. But then, it hadn't been nearly as exciting as one kiss from Jeff Hausen.

Scary thought.

"Diane? Toby and I are going to the hospital," Paul said as he stuck his head around the door. "Hey! Are you all right? You and Jeff didn't get in a fight again, did you?"

She straightened her shoulders. "No, of course not. I—I—was thinking about—about work."

"Oh. Well, Janie's asking to go with Toby. I told her no, but she cried and then Toby got upset. Can you think of something for her to do?"

"Yes, of course. We're going to the store and buy her a baby doll to play with. That will take her mind off Toby."

"Hey, doesn't Toby get a toy, too?"

"Yes," she agreed with a smile. "How about you? Do you want a toy?"

He grinned, not bothered by her teasing. "Nope. My toy is getting to play tennis tonight."

"I know," she agreed with a smile.

"Yeah. Jeff's the best."

She wasn't going there. "Ask Toby if he likes cars or airplanes or what. Okay?"

"Sure."

She followed him out of the kitchen to cheer up little Janie. And wished her own problems could be dealt with that easily.

JEFF WAS FREE WHEN Paul and Toby got to the clinic. For some reason he'd had a lot of cancellations this morning.

"Hey, guys, you're right on time. No problems at home?"

"No, Diane distracted Janie for us," Paul said.

"She wanted to come, too," Toby said, a frown on his little face. "When can she see Mama?"

Jeff knelt down by the little boy. "I'd let her come now, Toby, but she wouldn't understand, like you do. She's too little. She'd cry and it might upset your mother."

"Oh."

Jeff stood back up. "What's Diane using to distract Janie?"

Paul chuckled. "She's taking Janie to the store to buy her a baby doll. And Toby gets some cars to play with."

"Yeah," Toby said, beaming at him. "Diane promised."

"That's terrific," he assured Toby. Then he leaned closer to Paul. "Does she have any money?"

Paul looked surprised. "I guess so. She didn't say anything about it."

Jeff led them into Toby's mother's room. After a few minutes, he told one of the nurses where he'd be and hurried out to his car. He drove to the big bargain store on the edge of town—one of the few places that carried toys—and found Diane's car in the parking lot. After parking beside it, he hurried into the store.

Janie, instead of Diane, saw him as he came into the store. Toby had accidentally called him daddy several times, but Janie never had. Until now.

"Daddy!" she exclaimed in the almost empty store.

All the occupants turned to stare first at Jeff and then at Diane and Janie.

Jeff swallowed his groan. Diane wasn't going to be happy about his arrival. Already she was frowning fiercely.

When he got close, she whispered, "What are you doing here?"

"Can't I shop where I want to?" he demanded,

refusing to allow small-town gossip to limit his behavior.

His words checked Diane's anger. Almost. She
stared at him. "Okay, what are you shopping for?"

He didn't have an answer. Finally, he went with
the truth. "Paul told me—I wanted to make sure you
had enough money—you shouldn't have to pay for
everything."

Diane rolled her eyes. "I have enough money for
a toy for each of the children. Thank you, but go
away."

"I don't see why you get to have all the fun," he
insisted, irritated at his dismissal.

"Fun? Fine!" She thrust Janie into his arms. "I'll
go shop for things for me!" And she walked off.

"Where Di go?" Janie asked, staring after her.
Much like Jeff.

"Uh, she needs to shop. Are you ready to pick
out a dolly? Your dolly to take home with you?"
They were standing in the aisle filled with all kinds
of dolls, several bigger than Janie. He wondered if
she would choose the biggest she could. Apparently
she hadn't had too many toys. Would that be okay
with Diane?

He wished she'd come back.

"Down!" Janie announced and began squirming
in his arms.

He set her down and she immediately raced down
the aisle.

Jeff hurried after her. She certainly kept his attention. He didn't have time to think about Diane and

her behavior. When Janie finally chose her doll, a small one she could carry in her arms, he looked up to find Diane watching them.

"I'm glad you came back," he said.

Which got Janie's attention. She whirled around to find Diane and ran toward her. "Di! My baby!" She showed Diane the baby at length as Diane knelt down to her eye level.

"It's a very nice baby. What's her name?"

"Baby!" Janie announced, a glow of pride on her pretty face.

Jeff and Diane exchanged a smile that made him hope he was forgiven.

Then Diane stood and looked away. "We need to find Toby's racing cars."

"All right! That's more my style than baby dolls," he told her. In fact, it was. He'd studied boys' toys when he'd been little. His mother's illness drained what little money they had. He'd seldom received any toys.

He spent a long time comparing the cars. When he finally chose a set for Toby, Diane gave an exasperated sigh.

"And they talk about women shoppers!"

"I just wanted him to have the best ones."

Her expression gentled. "He'll love them. But don't you have patients this morning?"

"No. I had a lot of cancellations for some reason. I don't need to be back until eleven."

Diane stared at him, a stricken look on her face.

"What's wrong?" he asked, checking his watch.

No, it was only nine-thirty. He hadn't missed any appointments.

Diane didn't answer him. "Come on, let's pay for these things and go."

"Did you buy anything for yourself? I can pay—"

That same expression was on her face. "No! No, you can't buy anything for me."

"But Diane, no one would—"

"Are you crazy?" she demanded. "Everyone would know. It wouldn't take fifteen minutes before everyone in Cactus would know you were buying me—" She turned bright red and hurried down the aisle.

He caught her arm, unsure what was upsetting her so much. "Diane, you did get something." As she'd turned, he had seen a package under her arm, something pastel wrapped in see-through plastic. "I can—"

She came to an abrupt halt, probably having forgotten that she'd picked up something. She grabbed the package from under her arm and thrust it on the shelf nearest to her.

She continued ahead, but Jeff paused to read the label on the package.

Suddenly understanding, he followed her.

After all, she was right. He couldn't buy her underwear, bikini underwear, without giving a whole lot of people the wrong idea.

Himself, included.

Chapter Eight

When Jeff got home that evening, Diane had everything ready for their picnic. Janie had taken a nap
with her new baby in her arms. Paul had played cars
with Toby, until Diane had insisted Toby had to rest.

Paul had sat in the kitchen with her, helping make
deviled eggs and chatting. His arm scarcely hurt
anymore and he was optimistic about his tennis. Diane didn't care what he talked about as long as it
didn't include Dr. Jeff Hausen.

She couldn't get the man out of her head. Especially since she felt obligated to tell him why he'd
had so many cancellations today. The cashier's comments had explained it all to Diane.

It was possible Jeff would want them to move out
at once and she had nowhere to take her tribe. But
she couldn't blame him. His income was going to
suffer as long as the women in the community
thought he was involved with her.

"I wonder why Jeff hasn't remarried?" Paul
asked.

Diane's head jerked up and she stared at her brother. "I wouldn't know."

Almost as if she hadn't spoken, he continued. "I know some men like to be single so they can date a lot, but Jeff doesn't do that. And he's great with the kids. He should have a houseful."

She decided to check on the chicken rather than respond to that comment.

"Don't you think so?" Paul asked.

"He seems to enjoy the children, but I think it's a novelty."

"Maybe. He's awfully good with the patients, too."

Before Paul could continue, the phone rang. He looked at Diane. "Should we answer it?"

"I suppose so," she said, but she continued turning the chicken, so Paul moved to the phone.

When he hung up, he said, "That was Katie. When I told her about our picnic, she asked if she and Gabe could come. You don't mind, do you?" he asked.

"Of course not. Hmm, I'd better add—" She was mentally running down what supplies she had, when Paul interrupted her.

"Katie said she'd bring food for them. For you not to worry. Besides, Di, you always fix more than we can eat."

She shrugged. "It makes a good lunch the next day."

So she packed the food, dressed the children after

their naps and had everything ready for them to go to the tennis courts.

"I came home early to help," Jeff said as he realized all was prepared.

She thanked him for his thoughtfulness, but she didn't look at him. She'd experienced a little too much of Jeff Hausen for one day. Especially if they were going to keep their distance.

"So, we're all ready?" Jeff asked and received enthusiastic replies from the other three.

"Baby go," Janie told him, holding up her new doll.

"You bet," he assured her, swinging her and Baby up into his arms. "How about you, Toby? Are you taking your cars?"

"No, I'm 'fraid I'll lose them. Paul played with me today and we had fun."

"Good."

Diane felt his gaze on her and for the first time in her life she felt self-conscious in her modest cut-offs. But it was too warm to wear long pants on their little picnic.

Once they reached their destination, Janie and Toby went to the swings. Diane grabbed the picnic basket to follow only to find Jeff's hand covering hers. She snatched her hand back.

"I can carry that. It's too heavy for you to—"

"I'm strong enough! You—you go play with Paul," she said, hating the fact that his touch affected her breathing.

"Paul can wait."

She glared at him, then turned away. He wouldn't be so friendly when he discovered they were hurting his income.

Deciding to get the moment over with, she said, "I know why you had so many cancellations today."

He stopped walking and turned to stare at her. "What are you talking about?"

She walked around him so she could supervise the children. "The lady at the grocery store said women were pretending to be sick so they could— could meet you. And that once word got out that you and I—I mean, that we were an item, she supposed they would stop coming. I'm sorry. If you want us to move out, I'll try to find—"

He put the picnic basket down where he stood and grabbed her arm, halting her progress. "You're kidding."

"No, I'm not."

"You think I'd dump you on the street because of a bunch of silly women?"

"I told you Cactus is a small town. You'll lose a lot of money just because— There's a lot of matchmaking going on."

"I know, but I told them to stop. I mean, Mabel and Florence, Ruth and Edith. I made it clear I didn't want—"

"Why did you do that? It's obvious you'd like to have a family. Paul said so today." That thought had stayed with her all afternoon.

"Our 'family' is temporary."

"So you don't want children?"

He stepped closer. "I didn't say that."

Diane wanted to move away, but she refused to let him intimidate her.

Just as she was sure he was going to say something else, Paul hollered at them and threw a tennis ball. It bounced up and hit Diane in the back and she stumbled in surprise—right into Jeff's embrace.

To find herself in his embrace so soon after this morning's kiss left Diane stunned. Before she could pull herself together and move away, his head began to lower. He was going to kiss her again!

"Hey, are we interrupting?" Gabe called as he and Katie approached.

Even as Katie elbowed her husband, Diane and Jeff jumped apart.

"Uh, no. I stumbled because our little brother hit me with a tennis ball," she breathlessly informed Katie. "I'm glad you could make it," she added, pasting a big smile on her face, hoping they wouldn't notice her red cheeks. "Is Mom taking care of the baby?"

As Katie nodded, Paul jogged over to say hello and apologize for the tennis ball.

Jeff wiped the surprise off his face and extended a welcome, then added another as he saw Cal and Jessica approaching. "I didn't know we were having company."

Katie said, "I hope you don't mind. After I talked to Paul, I called Gabe and he told Alex and Mac and suddenly, we had a crowd."

Diane turned around to see a lot of their friends gathering. She only hoped they hadn't seen Jeff holding her. That wouldn't help Jeff's appointment schedule. Or her reputation. "Of course we don't mind. Hi!" she called, waving to the others.

Jessica and Cal had brought Rick, their oldest, just about Janie's age, as had Alex and Tuck and Spence and Melanie. Those three had all been born on Mac and Samantha's wedding day. Samantha's daughter, Cassie, was closer to Toby's age. Each of the new babies had been left with their respective grand-mothers.

"This was a great idea!" Jessica exclaimed as she spread out a blanket on the grass by the swings. The men had joined Paul and Jeff on the courts. "There's not a lot of choices for entertainment in our fair city."

"I like it that way," Samantha said. "It's a relief after Dallas."

"Don't you get bored?" Diane asked.

Her sister's sharp gaze focused on her. "Do you think you'll be bored here?"

Diane regretted her question. She didn't want Katie worrying about her. The entire family had relied on her big sister much too long.

"Give her a break," Alex said. "She's just set-tling in. I was a little worried about that when I married Tuck. But he takes care of the boredom," she assured everyone with a chuckle.

"Once you're married," Jessica assured her, "you'll be grateful for a quiet life."

Diane opened her mouth to assure the ladies she didn't intend to marry, but she caught Katie's eye and changed her mind. "Who knows? I may never meet anyone." Then she started searching for another topic of conversation.

The ladies didn't bite, however. Melanie stared at her, surprise on her face. "But Jeff—"

"Is temporarily housing us. It's very generous of him," Diane said, "but I'm afraid we're going to have to find somewhere else to go. His appointments are dwindling even as we speak."

Katie frowned. "What do you mean?"

"Now that we're staying with him, people are assuming we're—uh, an item and the ladies are cancelling their appointments."

Jessica laughed. "I know what you mean. Cal stopped getting so many frightened women calls when I hog-tied him."

The other ladies seemed surprised by Jessica's remark. Much to Diane's relief, the conversation shifted to courtship and the problems that complicated her friends.

Until the conversation turned to the matchmakers.

"You'd better be on the lookout for our adored mothers-in-law," Samantha warned. "The idea of a single woman and a single man with no marriage prospects seems to offend them."

"Can't you tell them I'm not interested?" Diane hurriedly asked.

The laughter grew even louder.

"You've got to be kidding," Alex said. "They

think they're the experts on matching people up. They certainly wouldn't pay any attention to us.''

Diane's hopes plummeted. Fortunately, the men returned from the tennis courts, hungry as usual. Everyone began putting out food, filling plates, feeding the children, and conversation became general.

Diane cleaned Janie's hands with a washcloth she'd brought with her. Jeff settled beside her and called Toby over.

''We're playing, Dr. Jeff,'' Toby explained with a frown.

''I know, but Diane needs to clean your hands so you can eat. You do remember her fried chicken, don't you?''

Toby grinned. ''Yeah.'' He stuck out his hands to Diane.

She looked at Jeff, lounging at her side, and tossed the washcloth to him.

''I think you can manage to clean up Toby. I'm fixing Janie's plate.''

''Watch it, Jeff!'' Cal said with a grin. ''She's roping you in.''

Diane glared at the sheriff before she turned her attention to Janie.

''I think she's teaching him an important lesson. Men can take care of children just as well as a woman can,'' Jessica said. ''Cal certainly knows that now, don't you?''

Cal didn't seem to mind her words. As the other men teased him, he proudly stuck out his chest. ''You bet. I'm the best dad in the world!''

"Hey, I thought I was," Tuck protested.

Alex turned on her husband. "You're the best at convincing your mother to take care of the kids."

He leaned over to kiss her neck. "Of course I am. How else will she get more grandchildren?"

Alex, the accomplished and wealthy lawyer, laughed even as her cheeks turned red. "I think two may be enough."

The teasing and laughter continued, but it didn't focus on Diane again, so she relaxed and began to enjoy herself. When she'd been younger, she had never run around with any of them because she'd been with friends her own age. But she enjoyed their company.

Jeff seemed to fit in well. He lay on his side next to her, slowly demolishing the plate of food he'd fixed himself. Janie leaned against his stomach, eating her own dinner, making a mess, of course.

Paul sat near them with Toby, who was sitting next to Cassie. The two of them seemed to be getting along well.

Maybe Cassie could come over and play one afternoon. Diane tucked that thought away for another day.

Samantha had obviously thought the same thing. "It's so nice for Cassie to have someone her own age to play with. How long will they be in town?" she asked.

Diane looked at Jeff. "At least several more weeks, right, Jeff?" After he nodded, she added, "I'd love to have Cassie come over to play."

"That would be great," Sam agreed. "I checked on Mrs. Duncan on Thursday. Any change since then, Jeff?"

"I think she's improving," he said casually, smiling at Toby's suddenly anxious face.

Samantha also noted the little boy. "I'm sure she is. Kids, if you're through eating, I bought some cookies at Katie's bakery. Anyone want one?"

Janie popped up at once. Only Jeff's fast reaction saved her plate from spilling. "Cookie!" she shouted and hurried toward Samantha.

"You've just discovered her favorite word," Diane told her friends.

"Maybe she's kin to Cal," Jessica suggested, grinning at her husband.

"Hey, just for that, lady, I'm going to beat you on the tennis court," Cal responded.

Jessica asked the others to watch her son and borrowed Jeff's tennis racket.

After they'd left the group, Diane leaned toward Jeff. "I thought you were going to play Paul some more?"

"Maybe later. I'll help keep an eye on the kids for a while. Besides, someone needs to help you clean up. That was a great meal, by the way. As usual."

"Gabe will play Paul," Katie said, obviously listening to their conversation. "It's too soon for me to run around since Rachel was born. I'm still feeling lazy."

"I'm glad you're following your doctor's advice," Jeff said with a grin.

Since he was the doctor in question, Katie chuckled. "Gabe made notes when we came in for the three-week checkup. Our next appointment is Tuesday."

"Good, at least I'll have some customers," Jeff said.

Samantha leaned forward. "Diane said it's finally happened. It's about time."

Diane stared at her. "You're happy about it?"

Samantha smiled. "Neither of us moved here to be run off our feet. Jeff has been tied up with those silly visits when we wanted to plan a push for school shots and public health classes. You know Florence planned those pregnancy classes and she likes to have one of us at every meeting. It's gotten a little hectic, especially when I had Charlie."

Diane turned to stare at Jeff.

"She's right," Jeff told her. "She warned me when I first got here, but I didn't believe her. Looks like I owe you one for ending those visits. I didn't realize it would happen so fast, though. I was a little surprised."

"You'll make less money," Diane warned.

"I have enough money," Jeff said, his voice casual. "The only thing I'm worried about is putting on weight. I haven't ever eaten this well."

"You mean since your mother cooked for you," Jessica said with a chuckle.

Jeff's grin disappeared. "No. My mother was sick

most of the time. She never cooked much.'' There was an uncomfortable silence until Jeff added, ''I wasn't malnourished, so stop looking at me like I'm an abused puppy.''

''Oh, I forgot to tell you,'' Katie suddenly said. ''Jack, our stepfather, is going to give us one of his pups to be raffled off at the Fourth of July celebration!''

Jack bred German shepherds. Gabe had gotten one when he came back to Cactus. Cinnamon, Gabe's dog, was the family pet now.

''That's wonderful,'' Diane exclaimed. ''That should raise some money.''

''True,'' Alex agreed. ''Almost all the business owners are contributing something. Jessica is donating a dinner for four at The Last Roundup.''

Samantha grinned. ''Jeff suggested we give school shots for a dollar contribution. I don't think that will make us very popular with the kids.''

''But the parents will appreciate it,'' Jeff insisted.

''True, but they'll like Diane's offer better,'' Katie said, grinning.

Diane turned a puzzled gaze at her sister. ''What offer?''

''The kissing booth, of course! The line will be long.''

''I didn't offer that! That was Jeff's idea,'' Diane protested, turning to glare at the man.

Melanie smiled. ''Maybe because he wants to be a customer.''

''I was just trying to be helpful,'' Jeff protested,

but he was grinning, and Diane wanted to smack him.

"Besides, Diane, the grocery store is going to sell breath mints, sort of as a sponsor," Alex added. "That should raise a lot of money *and* make your job more pleasant."

"You're serious? It's early. Can't I volunteer for something else? I could, uh, write wills or—or bake something or— I know. I'll run a baby-sitting booth, where people can drop off the babies while they have fun!"

"'Fraid not," Alex said. "Our insurance would go sky-high to cover child-care."

"We have insurance?" Diane asked in amazement. The plans seemed to have been rushing ahead without her knowledge.

"Of course," Alex said. "Our mothers-in-law have given all their time and talents to the organization of this event. And you know how thorough they are," she added with a big smile. "After all, the results are all eating cookies." She looked pointedly where the children were gathered.

Diane didn't want to do a kissing booth. But it seemed everything had already been arranged, thanks to Jeff Hausen. Well, she wasn't going to suffer alone. "I don't think it's fair to only offer a kissing booth for the men. I bet if we recruited some sexy hunk of a guy, we'd make a lot more money."

"Ooh! What a great idea," Melanie said.

"Yeah, like Spence would let you kiss another man," Jeff pointed out, grinning.

"No, I wouldn't but—"

"Me, neither," Katie said.

"Nor us," Alex added, including Samantha. "But that doesn't mean we don't have women who would. I think Diane's right."

Diane was pleased. Now it was time to lower the boom.

"He'd have to be handsome and single. You know, just to fulfill everyone's fantasy." She turned to stare at Jeff who, if she were judging by his expression, had just figured out where she was going. "Since it was Jeff's idea, and he fulfills those requirements, I think it's only fair he work in the kissing booth, too."

Jeff started protesting at once, but the ladies had come to a consensus before he got very far.

"But I have to help give the shots!" he exclaimed, turning a beseeching look on Samantha.

"Only one of us will work at a time, Jeff," Samantha said, a teasing look in her gaze. "That will leave you plenty of time to be in the kissing booth. In fact, I think we should have two couples, one to relieve the other. And maybe some people will buy kisses from each one."

Jeff, still looking uneasy, said, "You'll probably get a lot of men volunteering. I don't want to corner the market on fun assignments."

"Don't be so self-sacrificing, Jeff," Diane said, her voice filled with mock concern.

He leaned closer. "You're going to pay for this!" he hissed in her ear.

"Oh, really?" she whispered in return. "What can you do to me? Other than throw us out, and you promised you wouldn't do that."

"What are you saying?" Samantha asked. "No secrets around here."

"Secrets? He was threatening me," Diane revealed, sparing him a challenging look.

Jeff took a lot of teasing from the other ladies, and Diane enjoyed every minute of it.

The others returned from playing tennis. Paul was beaming, so Diane assumed his arm hadn't given him any problems.

Gabe sat down beside Katie. "This brother of yours is a demon player," he said.

"Did you lose?" Katie asked, all sympathetic.

"I slaughtered him!" Paul boasted with a big grin.

"Watch it, Paul. People are in a revengeful mood around here," Diane warned.

"Only you," Jeff added.

"Hey, that's it!" Katie exclaimed.

"What?" Gabe asked with a frown.

"Paul can be the other guy in the kissing booth," Katie said. "That will attract the younger crowd."

Jeff groaned. "It was bad enough that I'm being forced to kiss strangers, but now I've been insulted, too. Katie's saying I'm old."

Cal roared with laughter. "You are old!" He reached over to punch Jeff in the arm. "Makes the rest of us feel good. You're a whole year older than us."

Jessica smiled. "If you're going to be in the kissing booth, there'll be a line, Jeff, and you know it. But I do think it's smart to have a college guy there, too."

"Wait a minute," Paul protested. "I didn't volunteer for the kissing booth. I thought I'd help Katie sell cookies."

"Did you think I volunteered?" Jeff asked, his voice incredulous. "We were *both* drafted."

"Oh. Well, maybe I'll seek revenge, like Diane said," Paul said, glaring at his big sister.

"Oh, me, too," Jeff said, smiling at Diane.

The hair on the back of her neck stood up at his stare. There was a look in his eyes that warned her to be prepared.

"What kind of revenge?" Tuck asked.

"Well, I'm going to need to practice my kissing techniques. I figure it's only fair that Diane cooperates with me since it's all her fault."

Chapter Nine

"I feel much better now," Edith announced at their next planning meeting.

Florence stared at her. "You've been sick?"

"Oh, no! I mean about Diane and Dr. Jeff."

"Why? Didn't Diane call you to see if she could stay with you?" Mabel asked.

"Yes, she did, and I felt terrible about turning her down. But after last night, I think we may be right about them."

"What happened? And why haven't we heard about it?" Ruth demanded.

"Why, the picnic last night. Didn't anyone tell you?"

The other three women looked at each other.

Mabel said, "No, no one told us. How did you hear about it? And what is it we should know?"

"I talked to Melanie this morning," Edith said, beaming at them, not hesitating to brag. "She's such a wonderful daughter-in-law. She tells me everything."

"But *what* did she tell you?" Ruth demanded.

"She told me that when they got to the park last night, Jeff was holding Diane in his arms."

"Aha!" Florence exclaimed. "We're making progress."

"Even better," Edith continued, "when they drafted Jeff to be in the kissing booth with Diane, he told her she'd have to be his practice partner, and she turned a bright red."

"My, oh, my," Ruth muttered. "We *are* good."

Florence held up her hand. "Let's not get carried away just yet. We've got a long way to go before we get them to the altar."

"I'm not sure it's a good idea for them to agree to let other people kiss them. You know our boys wouldn't have tolerated that with their ladies." Mabel frowned, thinking about the developments. "We want them kissing each other, not half of Cactus."

"But those won't be real kisses," Edith pointed out. "There are rules, you know. Those kisses will just be little pecks."

"I know, but—" Mabel broke off, still thinking.

"We've got work to do, ladies," Florence pointed out. "I'm going by the clinic after our meeting to visit that poor woman."

"But she's in a coma, isn't she?" Ruth asked.

"Yes, but George thinks it will be a good idea," Florence said. "Now, here's a list of booths for the festival, and a list of donations for prizes."

So the ladies got down to business.

THE NEXT DAY WAS Saturday and Jeff had the entire day free unless there was some emergency. While he could sleep late, he rose at his regular time. So he headed for the kitchen to cook breakfast. It was time Diane got a break.

It also might soften her attitude toward him. After his teasing remark last night, she'd refused to speak to him, even after they got home.

And Paul wasn't any help. He was too irritated by his forced participation at the kissing booth. He scarcely noticed when Diane went to bed early, a book in her hand. He and Jeff ended up watching a guy movie by themselves.

When he reached the kitchen, his first task was to make a pot of coffee. He needed the caffeine. Then he cooked bacon. After mixing up the pancake batter, he heated the griddle while he cut up some fruit. He'd found strawberries and grapes in the refrigerator and bananas on the counter.

He was putting batter on the griddle when the kitchen door swung open. Diane stopped abruptly, as she discovered him in the kitchen.

"Diane, you can't still be mad at me. Come on in and have some breakfast. I've got everything ready." He watched as she considered his words.

"Don't think I've forgiven you," she said, her voice gruff. "You embarrassed me in front of my family and friends." But she did enter the kitchen and sit down at the table.

He poured a mug of coffee and carried it to her. "I know, but I don't see why that was so embarrassing. I was just kidding. And it's not like you've never been kissed before.''

Returning to the stove, he flipped the pancakes before taking a plate out of the cabinet.

Diane got up again and he feared she was leaving. "Diane!"

"I'm just getting the syrup. You forgot to put it on the table.''

"Oh. Sorry.'' He handed her the plate of pancakes and immediately poured more batter on the gril. He was looking forward to sharing a quiet meal with her. He'd just gotten to the table with his breakfast when they both heard the children stirring.

"I was hoping—I thought the kids would sleep in,'' he finished lamely.

"Are you losing your enthusiasm for children? They never sleep in when you want them to,'' Diane said, staring at him.

"No, I still want kids but that doesn't mean I don't like adult time, too.''

Diane took a bite of her pancakes. After chewing, she said, "I thought you had adult time last night after the kids went to sleep.''

"With Paul? That wasn't what I had in mind.''

Just then, Toby and Janie entered the room. Janie ran to Diane to crawl up in her lap and give her a hug. Toby, too, crossed to Diane's side and hugged her before he sleepily sat down.

"Hey! What about me? Don't I get a hug?'' Jeff asked. It pleased him when both children hurried to his side and gave him a hug. True, Janie went back to Diane, but she did give him a hug. That was progress.

He got up and fixed their pancakes. "Do you think Paul is ready for breakfast?" he asked Diane.

Toby answered. "He was waking up, but he said he was going to take a shower first."

About that time, they heard the shower shut off, so Jeff made pancakes for Paul, too. By the time he brought them to the table, Paul joined them.

"Thanks, sis, this looks good," Paul said as he sat down.

"Don't thank me. Jeff made breakfast today."

"I thought you deserved a break," he said.

She gave him a wry smile. "You were hoping cooking breakfast would get you off the hook."

Paul frowned. "Did you two have a fight?"

"Not really," Jeff said. "But your sister volunteered me for the kissing booth, remember?"

"Yeah, so you should be mad at her," Paul pointed out, "not the other way around."

"Yeah, Diane," Jeff agreed with a grin.

She gave him a knowing stare. Then she turned to her brother. "I don't know why you're objecting to being in the kissing booth. What better way to meet all the young ladies?"

"Hey, I hadn't thought of that," Paul said. "But I have to kiss anyone who has a buck. Some of those old ladies love to pinch my cheeks. I can just see them lining up with their dollars."

Diane shrugged her shoulders. "You have to kiss

a lot of frogs before you find a prince. Or in your case, a princess.''

"How many frogs have you been kissing?" Jeff asked. He had a lot of questions for Diane, but he figured they were too personal for her to give him an answer. Maybe he could get some answers this way.

"I guess not enough," she said, avoiding his gaze. "After all, I haven't found my prince yet."

It struck Jeff that he might have found his princess. Whenever he got close to Diane, his heart raced and his breathing grew shallow. If only they wanted the same things out of life. He wanted kids, she didn't. He wanted to stay in a small town, she didn't. He wanted a woman who could spend as much time with family as she did with a career. She apparently didn't. How could something so perfect seem so wrong?

Paul shrugged his shoulders. "Hey, Jeff, want to play some more tennis this morning?"

Normally, Jeff would've been pleased with a tennis game on a Saturday morning. But not this Saturday morning. "Thanks, Paul, but I thought Diane might appreciate having her day free, so I'm taking the kids today."

"Oh."

Diane looked up. "I'm going to do some laundry this morning, Jeff. Why don't you go ahead and play tennis and then spend the afternoon with the children?"

"You sure you don't mind?" he asked, frowning.

"I'm sure. The kids are going to do a few chores, too, so they'll be ready to play this afternoon."

"Don't I get to go see my mama this morning?" Toby asked. "She'll miss me if I don't."

"How about I take you after my tennis game, just before lunch. Then we'll all go eat at The Last Roundup. How's that?"

Toby nodded and beamed at him.

Children were easy to please. He looked at Diane. "Okay with you?"

"Yes, if you think you can handle both children at the restaurant alone."

"I was planning on you going, too. And Paul if he wants. Then you can have the rest of the day off."

"Okay," she agreed, but there was no enthusiasm in her voice.

What had he done now?

HOW RIDICULOUS! DIANE scolded herself. Jeff was trying to be helpful—by shutting her out.

You don't want to play family, she reminded herself. *You told him that.* Yet, she longed to be included. Life was so confusing.

While the guys played tennis, she did several loads of laundry, including Jeff's dirty clothes. When she went in to strip his bed, she found a pile of dirty clothes in a laundry basket in one corner of the room. At least he hadn't left them all over the floor.

She had Toby and Janie removing the sheets from

their beds as part of their chores...with her help. She wanted the children to learn to be self-reliant. With a single mother, they would need to learn to help.

When the second load finished, she hung up Jeff's shirts and jeans so they'd be ready for him the next week. She'd noticed his rumpled appearance. Would he appreciate her work?

In between loads, she put clean sheets on all the beds, adding a spray of air freshener to the mattresses before she covered them. She gave Janie a feather duster and showed her how to dust the bedside tables in all three bedrooms being used.

Toby asked to dust too, so she had him dust the den while she and Janie set out cookies and glasses of milk as reward for all their hard work.

While they ate cookies, she added more laundry and folded the next batch of clothes. Then she laid out the children's best clothes and sent them to dress.

A very productive morning.

But it hadn't done much to keep her mind off Jeff. Thoughts of him colored every moment, especially since she was in his home. It was such a family home, too. Strange for a single man. Of course, he'd made it clear he intended to have a family some day. He'd better start soon, since he was already thirty-five.

She smiled as she pictured his reaction at that statement. He was a little sensitive about his age. But he had no reason to be. His age was perfect for most women wanting to start a family. It would be perfect for her, too, but, of course, that wasn't what she wanted.

"So why did you react so strangely at breakfast?" she asked herself.

"We're ready, Diane!" Toby called.

She'd been putting away clothes when he called. She hurried down the hall to check out their appearances, glad she could compliment them. "You look wonderful. Just let me brush Janie's hair." The little girl's blond curls reminded her of the times she'd brushed Susan's hair when they were all going to church on Sunday mornings.

After giving Janie a hug, she led them to the den and put in a Disney video to entertain them until Jeff and Paul returned.

They came in the back door as she came out of the den.

"Hi, honey, we're home?" Jeff said. "I'm safe saying that, aren't I? I don't see any loaves of bread around."

She grimaced. "There are other things I can throw, Dr. Hausen, so I wouldn't get too bold, if I were you."

"Yeah, and Di played on the softball team," Paul added, grinning. "She's dangerous."

"Definitely," Jeff agreed, but his voice had lowered and he stared at her.

Diane was pretty sure he was thinking about something other than bread loaves. She changed the subject. "The kids are all dressed and ready. You need to take your showers quickly before they get bored with the television.''

"Yes, ma'am," Jeff agreed with a swift salute. Then he and Paul raced up the stairs.

Diane drew a deep breath and went into the kitchen to pour herself the last of the morning's coffee. It still tasted halfway decent, especially when she added a cookie or two.

JEFF ENTERED HIS BEDROOM and immediately knew Diane had been there. Not only was there a lingering scent he associated with her, part spicy and part sweet, but the bed was made. Even more telling, his laundry basket was empty of all the dirty clothes. He opened his closet and found them neatly hanging there.

He hadn't intended for her to clean up after him. Reminding himself to thank her but let her know the extra work wasn't necessary, he turned on the water in the shower and stripped while it was warming up.

A few minutes later, he entered the kitchen to find her sipping a cup of coffee.

"Hey, Diane, thanks for cleaning my bedroom and clothes, but I didn't intend for you to wait on me. That's too much for you to do."

"I did them with everyone else's. Don't worry about it."

He frowned. "Look, I mean it. I don't want you feeling like Cinderella. In fact, I should hire a housekeeper since you're going to start work on Monday."

"There's no need for that," she said sharply. "I'm paying you for having us with my housekeeping. Remember?"

"No! I don't need payment to help out in an emergency. That's how small-town people react."

"We also don't take charity," she said firmly, feeling unwelcome when he talked about hiring someone to do her chores.

"What are we arguing about?" Jeff asked, frustrated. "I can hire a housekeeper if I want one. And you've got other things to do. I just wanted to say thank you."

"A simple thank-you is enough. There's no need to hire someone to do what I can do."

"A simple thank-you, huh?" He settled his hands on her shoulders and pulled her to her feet. "Okay, here's a thank-you." Then he covered her lips with his, wrapped his arms around her until he couldn't tell where he started and she finished.

The hunger that had been building in him since he'd first tasted her lips exploded. His hands explored her slender body, urging her closer. He lifted his mouth to reslant it over her lips, to take the kiss deeper. He plunged his tongue into her mouth. To his pleasure, she met him more than halfway.

With such encouragement, he forgot where they were or why they shouldn't be wrapped in each other's arms. All he could think about was Diane…and carrying her up to his bed.

Before he could get enough of her, if that would

ever happen, Paul entered the kitchen, Janie and Toby at his side.

"Hey! What's going on?" he asked.

Paul's words seemed to awaken Diane from whatever state she was in, a cooperative one, Jeff realized regretfully.

She stared at her brother, shock on her face.

"We were praticing for the kissing booth," Jeff announced, trying to control his breathing, his gaze fixed on Diane.

"I don't think you'll have to kiss anyone like that," Paul assured them both with a big grin.

Jeff ignored his words and Diane hadn't spoken at all. He looked at the kids. "Ready to go? You both look very nice."

Janie hugged his knees. "I dress myself," she assured him.

"And you did a great job. Let's go see your mama," he said, trying to get them moving before Paul said anything else that would embarrass Diane.

"Mama?" Janie shrieked. She turned to her brother and repeated that one all-important word. "Toe, Mama!"

"I know, Janie. Mama's sleeping, though. She can't talk to you."

The child stared at her brother, then turned to Diane. "Mama?"

Diane bent over and picked her up. "Yes, Mama. Dr. Jeff is going to take us to see her."

Janie reached for Jeff, as if she had to be carried

by him or she would miss the opportunity to see her mother.

He took her, brushing against Diane's arm as he did so. He saw a reaction in her eyes, matching his own. Touching Diane increased his heart rate, no matter how casual it was.

"Are we taking the SUV?" Paul asked, turning to go, holding Toby's hand.

Just as Jeff agreed, Janie screamed again, but this time her word was "Baby!" She began struggling to get down.

"She wants to take her doll," Diane clarified.

Jeff put her down and told her to hurry.

Paul told them he'd take Toby out to the car. Suddenly they were alone again.

Diane stood a step back from him.

"Di, I didn't mean to—I really did want to say thank you."

"I don't think that's a good way," she mumbled, looking away from him.

He couldn't resist teasing her. "I thought it was spectacular. You're easy to kiss."

Her shoulders straightened and she glared at him. "Well, if you're going to hire a housekeeper and thank her for her work that way, you'll have a long line of applicants!"

"Does that mean you liked it?" he asked, grinning.

She stomped her foot. "Stop teasing me!"

"Ready!" Janie announced as she returned, her doll clutched in her arms.

"Good," Diane said to her. "Then let's go."

Her enthusiam depressed Jeff.

DIANE WAS GLAD TO GET out of the house. There would be no more opportunities for Jeff to—no, she'd best not think about that kiss. Or she might be pleading for time alone with the man. He was going to earn a fortune in the kissing booth.

When they reached the clinic, she could sense the tension rising in Toby. It made her wonder if the visits were good for the little boy. Janie was unaware of what awaited her.

The building was small and Jeff, of course, knew everyone working there. Diane knew most of them, she'd even gone to school with several. Their progress was slow as everyone stopped to chat.

Diane wouldn't have minded talking about old times. But the most popular topic stunned her. All the nurses wanted to talk about Jeff's unwrinkled shirt. Diane was congratulated on taking good care of "her man."

When she first tried to protest, to explain, she was teased even more. Finally she gave up. Jeff watched her, apology in his gaze, but she knew by nightfall there would be no doubt that she and Jeff were a couple.

But she had other things to occupy her mind. Janie began to pick up on her brother's tension. She hid her face against Diane's neck as she carried her. When they reached the door of their mother's room, Toby turned again to warn his sister.

Paul led Toby into the room. Jeff put his hand against Diane's back and guided her and Janie into the room. The little girl looked at her mother and cried out "Mama!" but the word was fearful, not happy.

Toby took his mother's hand and began talking, telling his mother that Janie had come and Diane and…

And her eyes opened.

Diane gasped and looked at Jeff to see if he had noticed. He was staring first at the woman and then the machines. He picked up his patient's other hand.

Toby was staring at his mother's hand and didn't look up until he felt her move. When he saw her eyes open, looking at him, he, too, shouted one of Janie's favorite words. "Mama!"

Chapter Ten

Jeff asked Diane to take the children out of the room for a few minutes even as he pressed the button to summon a nurse.

"But I want to talk to Mama!" Toby protested.

"You will, honey," Diane promised. "But Dr. Jeff has to see if she's—if she's feeling all right." She held Janie on one hip and reached out for Toby's hand.

"I've got him," Paul told her. Together they herded the children out of the room.

Diane looked over her shoulder at Jeff as they moved away. His attention seemed to be focused on his patient, but suddenly he looked up and mouthed thank you, accompanied by a special smile.

Paul already had Toby in a chair in the waiting room, quietly talking to him. Diane joined them, holding Janie in her lap after she sat down.

Toby was full of questions. Janie only had one. "Mama?"

"Yes, sweetie, Mama is getting well. I think you'll get to see her in a few minutes."

Toby heard her. "We can talk to Mama?"

Diane hesitated. "I'm not sure, Toby. She hasn't been awake for a while. She may be really tired. But I think Dr. Jeff will let you at least see her."

"Mama!"

"But she shouldn't be tired," Toby said with a frown. "All she's been doing is sleeping."

"It's a very good thing that she woke up," Diane said, smiling at Toby, "But when you haven't, uh, used your muscles in a while, it makes it difficult to get everything working again. Your mama will have to stay in the hospital a while longer."

"Oh," Toby said, disappointment in his voice.

Janie, of course, didn't understand what Diane had said. Her only question was the same. "Mama?"

"Mama's getting better," Diane assured her.

"Yes, your mama is getting better," Jeff said, suddenly appearing. "Now, I'm going to let you and Janie go see your mama for just a minute. Then we have to let her go back to sleep." Jeff held out his hand to Toby.

Toby slid out of his chair and took Jeff's hand. "But will Mama wake up again?"

"Yes, she will, just like you do every morning."

Diane had wondered the same thing, so she was as relieved as Toby. Jeff smiled at her, a tender smile, as if he understood her fears as much as he did Toby's.

He really was wonderful with the children. And her. She hated to admit it, but she knew if something was wrong with her or her family, she'd put all her trust in Jeff.

"Paul," Jeff added, "why don't you go to The Last Roundup and get us a table? We'll be there in a couple of minutes."

With a grin, Paul headed out the door.

Jeff led the children into Evie Duncan's room.

Toby gently hugged his mother and kissed her cheek. "Mama, Janie's here, too," he added. "Diane's holding her."

Diane stepped forward so Janie could touch her mother. The child tried to leap into her mother's arms, but Diane held her firmly. "I'm Diane Peters. I'm—we're taking care of Toby and Janie until you're well."

"I'm so—grateful," the woman whispered, her eyes tearing. "I can't—"

Jeff stepped forward. "There's nothing you need to do except get better. We've got everything covered."

"I don't even know where we are," she returned, the tears now streaking down her cheeks.

"You're in Cactus, a small town about an hour from Lubbock. You don't need to worry about anything," Jeff said again. "I'm going to give you some medicine to sleep again, so you'll get stronger. The best thing you can do is relax," Jeff added, using that winning smile of his.

The nurse arrived with a pill and Jeff lifted Mrs. Duncan briefly so she could drink water.

"We're taking Toby and Janie to lunch, so you just rest. They'll be back soon for another visit."

Jeff ordered the nurse to stay with her until she fell asleep. Then he took Toby's hand and led him out of the room. Diane and Janie followed, but not quietly. Janie reached over Diane's shoulder and cried out for her mother.

When they got out of the room, Jeff took Janie from Diane's arm as the little girl continued to struggle. "Toby, can you escort Diane?"

Diane watched the little boy wipe his face to rid himself of tears and square his shoulders. Then he reached out for Diane's hand. "I don't know where we're going," he told Jeff with a frown.

"Diane does. She'll show you," he said. Then he cuddled a reluctant Janie against his shoulder. "Come on, sweetheart, let's go eat. I think they have ice cream at this restaurant. Do you like ice cream?"

Having expertly given each child something to think about other than their mother, Jeff escorted them to lunch.

JEFF ENJOYED HIS LUNCH, buoyed by Mrs. Duncan's sudden awakening. While she'd have to remain in the hospital for several weeks, he could now say with some certainty that she would fully recover.

His gaze traveled over the two children. Janie was eating her lunch in order to get the ice cream he'd promised. Toby was behaving perfectly, but Jeff could see the worry in his gaze.

He leaned forward. "Toby, your mama is going to be okay. It will take a little time, but everything's going to be okay."

The little boy nodded.

Diane, sitting beside Toby in the booth, put her arm around him and hugged him close. "Dr. Jeff wouldn't lie to you, Toby."

"I know."

Jeff's attention was diverted to Diane. Hearing her praise him was wonderful. A few days ago, she'd barely speak to him and she never smiled. Things were improving. He'd discovered they could communicate without words.

His mind immediately flew to the ultimate communication, the kisses they'd shared. He kept his gaze lowered, afraid she'd realize what he was thinking about.

But they still had the difficulties about her choices. They wanted the opposite things. He couldn't believe she'd prefer the anonymous big city to Cactus.

Already, half the town had stopped by to greet them. Of course, they'd also addressed them as a couple. That didn't bother him, but he'd noticed Diane grew more and more withdrawn.

"Ice cream!" Janie announced, calling his attention to her plate.

"Okay. You did a good job with your lunch." He waved to the waitress.

When she arrived at the table, Janie announced her requirement at once.

After the waitress left, Jeff leaned forward to say, "I think Janie's got this ordering thing down."

"Mama says she's too demanding," Toby announced.

"True," Diane said with a smile, "but sometimes that's the only way you can get what you need. Besides, Janie's so cute, no one minds."

"That never works for me," Paul joked.

"You're not as cute as Janie!" Diane assured him with a grin.

Jeff smiled, but he thought Diane could afford to be as demanding as little Janie, even if she wasn't. She was beautiful.

When they reached home, Diane immediately announced it was nap time for Janie. And she suggested Toby should lie down and let Paul read a book to him. After the other three left the room, Jeff protested. He'd intended to spend the afternoon with the children. "I can read to Toby."

"Of course you could, but I thought it might be good for Paul to rest a little while, too," Diane returned softly.

"What happened to me taking care of the children this afternoon so you can have some time to yourself."

"Do you remember Janie ordering her ice cream?" ·

He frowned. Of course he did, but what did that

have to do with anything? Nodding, he stared at Diane.

She drew a deep breath. "Well, I don't want to spend time by myself. I'll be working Monday afternoon. Then I'll be by myself."

Before he could think about her explanation, she asked another question. "Do you think it's a good idea to let Janie visit her mother again?"

"I don't think Janie was too upset, as long as we can afford more ice cream," he said with a grin.

"I'm not thinking of Janie. I'm thinking of Mrs. Duncan. The last thing she heard was Janie pleading to stay with her mother. That's got to be upsetting."

"Hmm, that's good thinking, Di. I hadn't thought of that. Maybe we'll just take Toby to see her for a few days and then reevaluate."

She stared at him, a surprised look on her face.

"What?" Had he done something wrong?

"Nothing," she hurriedly said. "I—most doctors aren't interested in listening to someone else's opinion."

"You've been hanging out with the wrong kind of doctors," he said. "Probably city doctors."

"Why are you so against big cities?" she demanded. "They're exciting. Something's always going on."

He stepped closer, his hands closing over her shoulders. "They're lonely."

"I've lived in Lubbock for six years. I wasn't lonely," she said sharply, staring at him.

"But weren't you sharing an apartment with your sister, Raine?"

"Well, yes, but I had friends, people in my classes."

"Were they friends? Or acquaintances who shared similarities because you were in class together. How many have you talked to since you came home?"

"I haven't been home long," she protested.

"I know. I had a lot of friends at the hospital in Houston. But I never saw them except at work." They were people he liked, but they all had their own lives.

"Your wife—"

"No. We weren't close."

She stared at him. "How can you not be—"

"She had a career."

Diane blinked several times, staring at him, and he wanted to kiss her…badly.

"A career doesn't mean you can't be close with your husband or wife. Look at Katie and Gabe. Or Jessica and Cal or—"

"I know, they all disprove my experience. But whose side are you on? I thought you would understand. After all, you want a career and no marriage partner." Was he finding a crack in her thinking?

She stiffened and tried to pull away from his hold. Her body was responding when it shouldn't. He liked to touch people. She'd already noticed how he used touch to communicate with people. Her cheeks flushed as she remembered how he touched her.

"I—we're not talking about me. I don't want the responsibilities. I've been responsible for other people since my dad died. Katie even more than me. She's happy with Gabe because she fell in love with him before—before she realized what was involved. I'm going to be smarter."

"But then you'll miss this," he whispered.

About to ask what he meant, she opened her mouth to speak. But before she could get any words out, his lips covered hers and he kissed her deeply.

He had a point, she thought fuzzily. His kisses were enjoyable, stimulating, exciting. Dizzying. And she wanted more, she realized. Her arms slid around his neck and she returned his kisses.

His response was flattering. He made Diane feel wanted, loved, special. The only lover she'd ever had hadn't made her feel that way. She realized now he had been more interested in his own pleasure. Jeff was a generous, considerate man. And sexy.

His lips drew her even closer and his hands slid beneath her T-shirt. As he touched her skin, it tingled and she wanted to return his touch, return the pleasure.

Then the ringing of the phone brought her to her senses. Especially when the caller turned out to be her mother, a woman who'd given up all her choices to a man.

THE NEXT MORNING, sitting in church listening to the sermon, Diane thought about the time in Jeff's arms. Their embrace had lasted much too long…and not long enough.

Amazing how a connection could be established with touching, kissing…dreaming. She took a deep breath and resisted the urge to stare at Jeff.

She'd insisted she had to do more laundry yesterday afternoon…to keep her distance from Jeff. As if clean clothes were of the utmost importance.

She looked at Toby who was wearing a brand-new jacket and slacks. Yesterday after his nap, Jeff had taken the boy shopping for new clothes. He'd even bought a pretty little dress for Janie, along with some white patent shoes and frilly socks. The new wardrobe was due to Diane's mother inviting them to dinner after church today.

Jeff was a good man, she thought. He deserved the family he wanted. That's why she had to stop kissing him. They didn't want the same things. She shouldn't mislead him.

But he was definitely the best kisser she'd ever known.

JEFF FELT LIKE A FATHER. And a husband. Here they were in church, he and Diane, with Toby sitting between them. Little Janie was in the church's child care center.

And after church, they'd all go to his wife's family home for dinner. Actually, Katie's home, of course, since that was where Margaret and Jack were living. He hoped Diane didn't realize how accepting that invitation would look to the townspeople. The townspeople who already thought they were a couple.

He'd held his breath when Diane asked him about the invitation. Sunday dinner with the family. She had no idea how much he wanted to accept. But he'd left it up to her.

Her acceptance was good for another reason. They wouldn't be alone. He was having trouble keeping his hands to himself. Yesterday, he hadn't intended to kiss her. His first mistake had been putting his hands on her shoulders. Almost without thinking about it, he stretched his left arm around Toby, on the back of the pew, until his fingers could touch Diane.

She jerked at his touch and stared at him. He smiled, as if his touch was casual. Then he gave a quick prayer, asking for forgiveness for his distraction. He wasn't concentrating on the Bible verses being read.

He pretended he wanted Diane to know that Toby was dozing. She smiled at him, nodding, before turning back to stare at the minister. So he kept his hand resting on her shoulder.

Paul, on the other side of him, was also dozing a little. His chin dropped and he jerked himself upright and gave Jeff a sheepish smile.

He, Paul and Diane had watched a movie last night after the little ones had gone to sleep. Not a particularly good movie, but it meant Diane stayed in the den with him until it was over.

Suddenly the audience stood. Jeff jumped to his

feet, hoping no one noticed his inattention. Toby tugged on his jacket and he leaned down to hear his request.

Jeff leaned back against the pew and allowed Toby to slip between him and Paul. Then he shifted next to Diane. She started to ask him a question, but the minister began leading a prayer and Jeff took her hand in his.

When the prayer had ended and they were leaving the church, Jeff continued to hold Diane's hand, while he shook hands with others. Diane tugged on her hand, but he held it steadfastly, not allowing her to pull away.

"People are going to think—"

"I'm afraid I'll lose you in the crowd," he whispered. Jeff shook Doc's hand and told the older man, "Mrs. Duncan, the children's mother, awoke Saturday. She's making rapid improvement."

Doc expressed his pleasure at that news, and Florence assured Jeff she'd be back to visit Mrs. Duncan when he said it was okay. She'd already gone while the woman was in a coma.

"I think that might be a good idea. She has a lot of questions about her situation, even though I've told her not to worry. Maybe you can help her understand," he said in response.

Florence nodded. "And how are you managing, Diane? I heard you're going to go to work on Monday." Since Mac was her nephew and also the original member of the law firm, it wasn't surprising that she knew.

"We're doing fine. Toby and Janie are wonderful," she said.

"I could possibly baby-sit for a few hours if that would help out," Florence added.

"That's not necessary. Mother is going to stay with them while I work."

"Oh, good. I really do have a great deal to do. We've got to get going on building the booths. I believe Jack is going to actually supervise, but we've got to purchase supplies, locate people to work the booths. We appreciate you two volunteering to work the kissing booth. Oh, and you, too, Paul. Do you have any suggestions for a partner?"

"A partner?" Paul asked blankly.

"A girl to work with you. You know, we're doing one of each, like Diane and Jeff."

Diane watched as her brother's gaze suddenly took on a glow of interest. "I met someone in Sunday school this morning. She's new to Cactus. It might help her meet people."

"Oh, really? I bet you mean Elizabeth Hampton. Such a nice girl. Quite beautiful, too, though I'm sure you didn't notice." Florence's smile was wide but Diane didn't mind. She wasn't talking to her.

"Uh, yeah."

Florence patted the young man's arm. "Don't worry. I'll ask her. Is it all right if I give her your number so she can call you if she has any questions?"

"Sure. Uh, I'm still at Jeff's."

"I know. So generous of Jeff to take you in,"

Florence said with a smile, letting it sweep over Diane, her hand securely held by Jeff.

Diane immediately tried to tug her hand free. Instead of succeeding, all she did was draw Jeff's attention.

"Anything wrong?" he asked, looking at her, then Florence.

"No! Um, I think we need to go. Mom always has dinner ready at once."

She could've kicked herself when she saw Florence's eyes light up at that information.

"You're going to a family dinner? How wonderful. You'll enjoy dinner at the Peters's, Jeff."

"I'm looking forward to it," he said with a grin.

ONCE THEY WERE IN THE Suburban, Paul and the two children strapped into the second row of seats, Jeff noticed Diane wasn't talking.

"Anything wrong?"

"Other than the fact that you hung on to me as if I was Toby's age and might get lost? Which only confirmed the gossip that's going around? Of course not!"

He couldn't plead innocent. He'd never carry that excuse off. "It was a big crowd." That wasn't a lie.

"Not that big. I want you to behave yourself at dinner," she said in a low voice. Since Janie was chattering in the back seat about the other children she met at the church nursery, she didn't think Paul would hear anything.

"You're becoming paranoid," he said firmly, keeping his gaze on the road.

"I am not! Did you see the way Florence stared at our—your—hand-holding?"

"Hey, you were holding, too."

She glared at him. "I didn't think anything about it until I caught people staring! And then I tried to pull my hand away. But you wouldn't let me."

"Paul had Toby's hand. I didn't have anyone's hand to hold but yours."

"Just don't do anything like that at dinner," she warned as he pulled into the driveway at Katie and Gabe's house. Since they were living in Gabe's grandmother's house, it was much less pretentious than Gabe's income would lead one to expect.

Changing the subject, he said, "I heard Gabe is thinking about adding to the house."

Distracted by that information, she said, "I hadn't heard that. I suppose, if they intend to have more children, they'd need to." She opened the door and started to get out. "Remember what I said," she added.

Jeff was growing irritated that she insisted on treating him like a pariah. Holding hands wasn't that big a deal. He looked over his shoulder. "Paul, can you take the children in for us."

Diane stopped moving and stared at him. "Why?"

Paul, fortunately, didn't ask any questions. He and the children got out and hurried to the house.

"Because," he began, answering Diane's question. "You have to pay a forfeit if I'm to keep my hands off you all afternoon."

"You're being ridiculous. We don't normally—"

He didn't let her finish her protest. Pulling her across the seat, he wrapped his arms around her and took the kiss he'd been dying for ever since the last time he'd kissed her.

It wasn't that Diane didn't enjoy Jeff's kisses. Unfortunately, she did. But she didn't enjoy the speculation they caused. Her family must've all been hovering at the kitchen window while he extracted his price.

When she and Jeff finally arrived inside the house, they were teased about their tardiness.

"We needed to—to discuss something."

Gabe laughed. "Yeah, we usually have those same discussions, but we wait until it's dark."

Everyone seemed to think Gabe was quite a wit, except Diane.

"Actually," Jeff drawled, "we were practicing for the kissing booth."

Diane couldn't protest Jeff's explanation. Because she didn't have any other explanation for what had taken place. She certainly didn't want to confirm to anyone how much she enjoyed his kisses.

Chapter Eleven

Jeff smiled to himself as he drove his "family" home. What a great afternoon. Many of his dreams had been enacted today. A big family meal. Not just good food, but a mingling of generations, the coziness of family. After the meal, everyone but Margaret and Katie had joined in a softball game.

He and Diane had been on opposite sides so one of them would be with Janie at all times. Diane showed her how to be a cheerleader, and everyone laughed at her antics.

"You're happy?" Diane asked, pulling his attention to her.

"Yeah. Today was great."

"Yes, it was fun, but you and I are going to have a discussion later."

His eyes gleamed. "Wonderful! I love our discussions."

"Not that kind!" she snapped.

"Too bad."

"Jeff—"

"Hey," Paul called from the back seat. "What did you think of Susan's friend?"

"Probably not as much as you," Jeff drawled, a big grin on his face. Susan had invited a high school friend to join the family dinner.

"What do you mean?" Diane asked, looking at her brother over her shoulder.

Paul's cheeks were bright red. "Uh, nothing."

Jeff explained, "He couldn't keep his eyes off her. Good thing they weren't on the same team, or he'd have played third base with his back to the batter."

Paul protested, but Jeff insisted he was right. Maybe the reason he was so sure was he'd been keeping his eye on Diane.

"Do you like her?" Diane asked, staring at Paul.

"She's new to town. Florence suggested I ask her to be my partner in the kissing booth."

"That would be nice," Diane agreed.

Much to her surprise, Paul didn't second the motion. "I've decided not to."

"Why not?" Jeff demanded.

"Because I don't want her kissing a bunch of other guys," Paul protested.

Jeff almost threw on the brakes. He caught himself just in time before he practically threw everyone through the front windshield. How could he have been so dumb?

When he'd mentioned the kissing booth, it had been because he wanted to kiss Diane. He figured he could spend fifty dollars and have a great evening for himself, disguised as charity. Instead, he'd just made it possible for every man in the county to kiss Diane.

Diane, unaware of his change of opinion, said, "Boy, you must really like her if you're that possessive. How long have you known her?"

Time doesn't matter. Jeff was relieved to discover he'd thought those words, not said them out loud. Because Diane would've thought he was crazy. He'd registered her beauty at the wreck. By the time he found her at the fire, he'd come to admire her stamina, her good heart, her gentleness, her care of two small children.

After sitting with her at the breakfast table, he'd realized he'd like to do so for the rest of his life. But he'd fought that feeling. After all, as he'd told himself over and over, that wasn't what she wanted.

But he sure as hell didn't want a bunch of other men kissing her. They might try to convince her to change her mind. *He* should be the one to—

Aha! That should be his plan. He should be working on changing her mind. As Paul put it, he shouldn't be letting other people have the opportunity.

"Um, you know, Diane, I feel bad about forcing you into the kissing booth. There's a new nurse at the office. I think she'd like that opportunity. Do you mind if I ask her to fill in?"

He figured she'd enthusiastically accept his offer. Instead, she stared at him for several seconds. Finally, she said, "No, of course not. That would be fine.'' And she turned to stare out the window the rest of the way home.

THE CHILDREN WERE exhausted from their afternoon, and Diane put them in bed at once for a late nap. Even Toby didn't complain. In spite of his cast, he'd played today. When one of the older participants got a hit, Toby had been the designated runner. He'd been ecstatic.

So quiet filled the house as the children settled down to sleep. Diane returned to the kitchen for a soda, feeling quiet herself.

Jeff had been so eager to replace her. She guessed he'd figured he should look for a woman who wanted the same things he wanted. A nurse would be a good wife for Jeff. She'd understand his work. And maybe she'd want a family. Probably loved life in a small town.

And she felt pretty sure there would be no more "discussions," the kind Jeff liked. He'd be practicing with the nurse.

That was no reason for her to be depressed. She'd told him she didn't want any of those things.

Of course, a woman could change her mind, couldn't she?

She loved taking care of Janie and Toby. They were so sweet. Cooking was even fun. It wasn't as if Jeff treated her like a servant. He was always helping clean up and offering to do more. And he appreciated home cooking so much.

It had been so long since she lived in Cactus,

she'd forgotten the relaxing rhythm, good friends, family life. Since her mother married Jack and Kate married Gabe, their family seemed healed, whole again, like before her father died, only better.

She'd hate to move far away.

Maybe she could take a job in Lubbock and come home every once in a while. Even see Jeff and—and tell him hello.

She'd be interested in what happened with his new girlfriend, of course. It would be like stopping twenty pages before the end of a romance. She wanted Jeff to be happy, though she wasn't sure the nurse would do.

"Are the kids asleep?" he asked, walking into the kitchen.

"Yes. I thought I'd drink a soda."

"Good, I'll have one, too. You're not upset about the kissing booth, are you? I mean, you've been very quiet since I suggested— I thought you'd be pleased."

"Yes, of course. It was very thoughtful of you. Have you called the nurse?"

"Yeah. I just got off the phone. She was thrilled to accept. I guess you don't meet too many men in the doctor's office."

"Just doctors," she said quietly, studying her can of soda.

Jeff laughed. "Yeah, and fifty percent of us are female in Cactus."

She noticed he didn't eliminate himself romantically. Unable to say anything else, she nodded.

"What did you want to discuss with me?" he prompted.

She took a drink, giving herself time to think. "Nothing now. I think everything is settled."

"You wanted to complain about my skills as a pitcher?" he suggested, grinning.

"No, though that brushback pitch you threw came awfully close."

"That wasn't a brushback," he protested. Then he sheepishly grinned. "I'm just not very good."

"Good enough for a backyard game."

"It was fun. A family afternoon. I've always wanted one of those."

"Don't you have any brothers or sisters?"

"No. My mother had multiple sclerosis. They detected it after she gave birth to me. It progressed rapidly. Sometimes, it takes years to worsen, but my mom's case was unusual."

"That must've been hard on you and your dad, as well as your mom," she said, her heart hurting for the picture she envisioned of Jeff as a little boy.

"Wasn't hard on my dad. He walked out on us when I was three. I don't really have much memory of him."

"No!" Diane protested, unable to believe a man could be so cruel and self-centered.

"Don't get upset, sweetheart," he said, reaching across the table to hold her hand. "We made it okay. He paid child support and alimony. Not enough to support us, of course, but my grandfather was alive then. He shared what he had."

"So your father kept in touch?"

"No. He paid what the law said he had to. But it was more than a lot of families receive when the man walks out on his obligations."

"I know, but—"

"Toby and Janie are in the same position, only I don't think they're getting much in the way of help," he pointed out.

"That's why you've been so wonderful, taking them in, providing for them," Diane said, nodding, as if confirming something.

"It certainly was part of it. But I'm learning about supporting your friends and neighbors in a crisis. Cactus seems to be a terrific group of people." Then, with a wink, he added, "Of course, it didn't hurt that you're beautiful."

"Jeff Hausen! You're just trying to hide your soft heart."

Jeff was still holding her hand and he squeezed it softly. "I do have a soft heart, but it's not all self-lessness, Di."

She tugged her hand away. "I guess it's a good thing we won't need to practice kissing anymore."

He sat upright. "Wait a minute. Where did you get that idea?"

"I'm not working the kissing booth now. There's no need to practice." She tried to keep her voice even. She certainly didn't want him to know she liked his kisses.

"You may not be, but I sure am! I need some

practice. I'm counting on you to improve my technique.''

Heaven forbid that he improve! He'd have half the town in love with him if he did. She tried to ignore the sense of relief that she felt.

''Won't you be practicing with the nurse you've selected?''

''Nah. I don't even know her very well. I know you'll be honest with me. Besides, kissing you is fun.''

''Um, I'm not sure it's a good idea.''

''Kissing doesn't hurt anything. In fact, as a doctor, I'd say it's good for you.''

''I was just beginning to respect your medical skills,'' she said, arching one eyebrow at him.

''Come here and I'll demonstrate what I'm talking about,'' he suggested, grinning.

''Come there? Can't you just tell me?''

''Nope. A demonstration is worth a lot of words.''

Diane debated whether to follow his directions. Finally, she got up from her chair and came around the table, wondering exactly what he had in mind.

It didn't take long for him to show her. Taking her hand, he pulled her into his lap, wrapped his arms around her and kissed her.

When she came up for air, her breathing was rapid.

''See? It tests your heart.'' He laid his hand against her breast and her heart raced even faster as her breast beaded under his touch.

"Yes," she murmured in agreement, barely able to think.

He didn't seem to want a scientific discussion either since he drew her even closer and kissed her again.

His technique was definitely improving.

DIANE WAS PLEASED TO start work on Monday. She had the morning to do laundry, straighten up the house, fix lunch for her and the kids. Paul was off with some of his friends.

Jeff was at the clinic.

She hoped time spent without him would give her a chance to be rational about her feelings. Not only had they gotten cozy in the kitchen yesterday afternoon, he'd followed her with his gaze the rest of the evening. When she started up the stairs to bed, he'd given Paul some excuse and followed her.

"Di?" he'd called, catching her before she opened the door to her bedroom where Janie was already asleep.

"Yes?"

"I forgot something,"

"What?"

"To kiss you good-night."

As if that were normal. She stared at him, unable to think of anything to say.

He kissed her again, tenderly this time, before turning around and running down the stairs. She stood there, touching her lips, knowing she'd be dreaming of him.

This morning, he'd kissed her goodbye, a casual salute also given to Toby and Janie. As if he hadn't wanted to leave her out.

This kissing thing was getting out of hand.

Now she'd be able to concentrate on her work. Show that she was still career-minded. Show that she could handle whatever Jeff Hausen had to dish out and still keep to her plan.

Oh, Lord, she hoped so, she added in a silent prayer.

Margaret got there just as they were finishing lunch.

"Hello, dear. How are you doing?"

"Fine. Thanks for watching the kids. Gabe's anxious for the research I'm going to do."

"It's not a problem. I miss having little ones around. I'm ready for Rachel to grow, so I can play with her more."

Having spent Sunday with Margaret, the children were happy with her presence.

Janie, having listened to Margaret's comments, slid down from the table and disappeared. Diane stared after her, then started to follow her, when Janie reappeared with her doll. She put her in Margaret's lap. "Baby!"

"Oh, you sweet child. Of course this is Baby. We'll play with her. Maybe I'll take her measurements and make her a new dress. And one for you to match! Would that be all right, Diane?"

"Of course, Mom. Janie and Toby don't have a lot of clothes." Diane had promised herself when she earned some money she'd buy the children more clothes. But that might take a while.

"Now, off you go. We'll clean up," Margaret assured her.

Diane spent the afternoon at the law offices, enjoying its professional but casual atmosphere. Alex took a coffee break and asked her to share the pot with her.

"I know you've only been here a couple of hours, but do you like it?" Alex asked.

"Yes, I do," Diane assured her with a smile. "I've missed the mental challenge. And it's fun being here with you, Mac and Gabe. Do you find it difficult to work and take care of your children, too?"

"I thought it would be difficult. But Ruth, my mother-in-law, is a lot of help. And we've hired a housekeeper. She's wonderful with the children. Then when I get home, she cleans while I play with them."

"That sounds like a good arrangement," Diane said, remembering Jeff talking about hiring a housekeeper. Not for her, of course, because she wouldn't be living with him after a few weeks.

"I know this sounds bad," Alex said, "but staying home all the time doesn't…well, I need some mental stimulation. But here I can have it all."

"I know. I love Toby and Janie, but making beds and singing nursery rhymes isn't enough. But I always thought you couldn't have both."

"You couldn't in a big city. But here, the guys don't seem to mind. In fact, you and I could split a day, and we wouldn't have to add on another office.

Hmm, I hadn't thought of that. Are you interested in a half schedule?''

"No! Not at all. I need to make some money so when I leave Cactus, I can travel a bit before I take a new job.''

"You're really going to leave?''

Diane looked away. "Why, yes, of course. I told all of you in the interview.''

"I was just hoping you'd change your mind,'' Alex said with a smile. "Oh, well, we'll enjoy you for a year. And that's a long time. Who knows, maybe you *will* change your mind.''

Diane thought a lot about what Alex had said. But she did a lot of work, too. In fact, she got so involved in her research, she forgot the time. When Gabe came in at five, to see what she'd discovered, she realized she was an hour late getting home.

"Oh, Gabe, I'm sorry! I'm late. I told Mom I'd be home by four. Um, here are the notes I've made on the cases that I think will help you. Can you—''

Gabe just grinned and took her notes. "I'll manage. If I have questions I'll talk to you tomorrow afternoon. You are coming in, aren't you?''

"Yes, of course,'' she said as she gathered up her belongings and headed for the door. She rushed home, after debating whether she should call her mother to apologize or just get there as fast as she could. Margaret liked to have dinner ready for her husband at a certain time.

She didn't see her mother's car when she reached Jeff's home. Knowing her mother wouldn't have taken the children without leaving a note, she ran in to check the kitchen counter before she drove to Katie's house to pick up the kids.

As lovely as Alex's life was, Diane didn't have a housekeeper to cover for her. The children were her responsibility, and she'd blown it.

Which meant, of course, that dinner would be late. Jeff would come in tired and hungry and be disappointed in her. Paul would complain. The children would get cranky.

Probably, Jeff would ask her not to work until the children left since she wasn't being responsible. And she'd enjoyed herself this afternoon.

And that was the problem about being a working mother, or as near as she'd ever be. You couldn't put your work first. You couldn't do your best work.

Well, she wouldn't stop work. These weren't her children. She'd just watch her time better. That's all. She wouldn't quit. No matter what Jeff said. Maybe she could find that apartment she intended to rent. And she could take the children to her mother so she could fix dinner on time whether Diane got there or not. She'd manage.

She sailed into the kitchen, her mind made up, determined not to be trapped like some women were. Only to discover someone else standing at the sink, wearing an apron, delicious smells coming from the oven.

"Who are you?" Diane demanded, not liking someone else in what she'd come to think of as *her* kitchen.

Chapter Twelve

Jeff was on the floor playing with Toby and Janie in the den when he heard Diane's exclamation.

"I'll be right back," he assured the kids as he leaped to his feet. In spite of the kids' protests, he didn't hesitate. He hadn't intended for Diane to learn about the change he'd made this way.

As he came through the kitchen door, he realized Diane no longer seemed upset. She was smiling at Hannah McBride, his new housekeeper. Closer observation, however, revealed stiff shoulders and tension in her smile.

"Diane!" he exclaimed, smiling as he watched her closely. "I see you discovered my surprise."

Tension radiated from her as Diane turned slowly around. Her smile was tight. "Yes, I was telling Mrs. McBride how lucky you are to have found her." Then she headed to the door.

"Dinner will be ready in about ten minutes," the new housekeeper called.

Diane gave her a brief thank-you and kept on going.

Jeff didn't try to stop her. He didn't want to discuss anything in front of Hannah. "The kids are in the den playing, Hannah. Can you keep an eye on them for a few minutes?"

He scarcely waited for her nod before he chased Diane up the stairs. The door to her room was already closed.

Rapping on the door, he stood quietly waiting for her to respond.

The door didn't open, but he heard a quiet question. "Yes?"

"Diane, may I come in?"

Silence.

"Diane, I need to talk to you."

"I'm busy right now. We can talk at dinner."

He didn't think that was a good idea. Not in front of Hannah and the children.

So he opened the door.

Diane was methodically folding her meager wardrobe and stuffing it in the duffel bag Katie had brought over.

"What are you doing?" Jeff asked, keeping his voice calm in spite of the alarm he felt.

"Packing." She never looked up.

"Why?"

"The children and I are moving to Katie's."

"Why?" he asked again.

"Because you won't let me pay you to stay here, so we have to leave."

He pulled his hands from his pockets and turned her to face him. "I never asked for payment," he protested, as if he didn't understand what she meant.

"I was doing the housekeeping in return for you taking us in—and you know it! But apparently I wasn't doing a good enough job and you hired Hannah—I mean, Mrs. McBride."

"Now you're being ridiculous!" he exclaimed. "You are a terrific housekeeper and you know it. But you have to start work and you can't do everything!"

"Yes, I can! But since you don't want my services, we'll leave."

"I don't think Katie has room for all of you." Jeff knew she didn't and he had no intention of letting Diane go. But he thought he'd pretend to be reasonable.

"We'll manage." Her words were clipped, her chin up.

"*You'll* manage. The children are staying right here. Paul, too. There's no reason for them to suffer just because you're a martyr."

Those words sparked her anger. "I am not a martyr! How dare you say that! Just because I don't want your charity doesn't mean I'm—you make it seem like I'm being unreasonable."

"You are." He'd kept his voice calm, but his heart was racing.

Tears pooled in Diane's eyes and she wrenched from his hold and crossed the room to stare out the window.

He followed and slid his arms around her. "Di, we're in this together. I can't stop work, so why should you?"

"This is your house. And I'm the one who volunteered to take care of the children."

She actually sniffed instead of letting the tears flow. His wife had always won any argument by dissolving into tears—not fighting fair. He again turned Diane around to face him.

"Right now, unless you decide differently, Hannah will come at eleven and stay until seven. You'll have the morning to yourself, you and the kids. Then while they nap and watch television in the afternoons, you can work."

"Hannah—Mrs. McBride—doesn't mind those hours?"

"She said since her husband died, she'd been very lonely. If you don't mind, I told her she could eat dinner with us. Is that all right?"

"You don't have to ask me. It's your home. You make the decisions."

He noted some of her tension had eased. "It's our home, Di," he said. "As long as we both live here taking care of the children, you have as much say as I do."

She started shaking her head, but he added, "Just as if we were married and Toby and Janie were ours."

"Most men don't feel that way," she said, her voice nearly a whisper.

Trying to lighten the moment, to bring a smile to

her beautiful lips, he teased, "How would you know? How many times have you been married?"

"None," she said, but her tone wasn't conciliatory. "I loved my dad, but he never let Mom share in the decision-making. When he died, Mom didn't know how to make decisions. I'm not going to be helpless just because I don't have a man."

"Then we're agreed. We make decisions together," he assured her, but he felt he'd just learned an important key to Diane's thought processes. She was afraid of being dependent because it made her weak.

"Dinner's ready!" Hannah called up the stairs.

"Come on," he said with a grin. "Let's go see if Hannah is half the cook you are." He caught her hand and tugged her toward the door.

DIANE REALIZED Hannah McBride knew she'd been upset. The woman's apprehensive look when they entered the kitchen told her that. She set out to make Hannah feel welcome.

"Oh, thank you for getting the kids to the table, Hannah. Do you mind if I call you Hannah? It seems silly to be formal if you're going to be here every day."

Some of the tension eased from Hannah's face. "Of course not, Diane, I mean Ms. Peters."

"Hannah, I've known you for years and we just agreed not to be formal. Diane is fine." Then she looked at the kids, who'd been silently waiting. "Aren't Toby and Janie good kids?"

"The best," Hannah agreed, beaming at the children.

As Diane had said, she'd known Hannah for years, but the woman had never had children so Diane hadn't known how she'd feel about adding two children to her work. She breathed a sigh of relief.

"But, Hannah, *we*," she paused briefly to stare at Jeff, "want you to know you're not here to wait on the children. We want you to help them learn to take care of themselves."

"That's a good way to raise children," Hannah agreed, but she smiled at the children. "I'm sure they'll be good helpers."

Hannah cooked a lot like Margaret and dinner was delicious. Afterwards, Diane began clearing the table, but Hannah stopped her.

"That's my job, Diane."

Jeff said, "Clearing the table is everyone's job, Hannah, but we'll let you be in charge of the washing."

Hannah agreed but shoved them out of the kitchen as soon as the table had been cleared. "I'll do the rest before I go home. You two go spend some time with the little ones."

"Good," Jeff replied. "Toby and I haven't finished playing cars, have we?"

Toby enthusiastically agreed.

"While you're playing, I'll bathe Janie," Diane said.

By the end of the evening, everything seemed settled. Paul had called and said he was staying at a friend's house. Hannah had gone home, promising to return the next morning, and Diane had realized the advantage of having Hannah come, even if Diane did worry about Jeff bearing the added expenses.

Just as she was about to apologize to Jeff for her initial reaction, the phone rang. Jeff grabbed it before it could wake up the kids. "Hausen."

Diane knew at once he'd received an emergency call because he tensed, ready to react. "Yes. Don't move him. If you can find something, cover him. I'll be there at once."

Diane had already picked up his medical bag and handed it to him as he put down the phone.

He took it, surprise in his eyes. "Oh, thanks, honey. I don't know when I'll be back."

"Don't worry. We'll be here."

He leaned over and brushed his lips against hers, as if she would expect a goodbye kiss, and hurried out the door.

Diane stood there, staring at the door. He acted like they were married and she wasn't panicking.

Ever since she'd seen her mother fall apart, she'd panicked at the thought of being like her. Partly because she'd discovered she was like her in other ways. She found it satisfying to cook a good meal for an appreciative audience. She loved children, eager to cuddle them in her arms.

She deliberately had chosen a profession that would give her little time for those things. She told herself she didn't want to be married, to have children. She didn't want to live in a small town.

But she'd lied.

Now Jeff was showing her it really was possible to have it all. If the man was like Jeff, not like Tom, her college flame, who wanted her to turn into her mother, Little Suzy Homemaker, with no interest outside the home, willing to be taken care of, to have no opinions or ideas.

Was it really possible? Or was it because Jeff knew it wasn't a permanent arrangement? She shrugged her shoulders. It *wasn't* a permanent arrangement.

She settled down in the den, watching an old movie. Somehow, she couldn't go to bed until Jeff returned and she knew who had been hurt, and the outcome. After all, she might know the person. It was a small town. She wasn't staying up for Jeff like a loving wife.

No, not at all.

JEFF CREPT INTO HIS HOME, trying to be sure he didn't awaken anyone. He smiled wearily. Even though they were all asleep, it made him feel good that the house wasn't empty.

He intended to fix himself a pot of decaf coffee and a snack to wind him down. Wrecks, especially that late at night, got his adrenaline flowing.

Then he realized the television in the den was on. Was Diane watching something? His heart beat faster as he anticipated seeing her. There was only one lamp on in the corner of the room as he tiptoed in. At first he thought the room was empty. Then he discovered Sleeping Beauty.

Diane was stretched out on the sofa, sound asleep. After watching her for several minutes, he moved closer. Bending down, he brushed her soft lips with his, barely touching her.

Startled, Diane jumped up, the top of her head bumping into his chin.

"Oh, you're back! I'm sorry, did I hurt you?" she asked with a gasp as she rubbed the top of her head.

"No, how about you? I was just trying to wake you up. Time to go to bed."

She blinked at him, slowly pulling herself together. "What happened? Was someone hurt?"

He cleared his throat. "Uh, yeah. Go on to bed and get some rest."

"But was it someone I know? Someone in Cactus?"

"No, someone passing through on the highway." He figured that would be the end of her questioning. She stood and walked out of the room to the stairway with Jeff following. He would make sure she made it to bed before he unwound.

Diane only made it a couple of steps up the stairs when she realized Jeff wasn't following. "Aren't you coming to bed?"

Jeff almost spoke the truth. *I will if you'll let me hold you.* "I'm going to have a cup of decaf first."

Diane immediately turned around and headed for the kitchen.

"What are you doing?" Jeff demanded.

"Fixing you a snack."

Though he protested she didn't have to take care of him, she just kept on going.

By the time he joined her in the kitchen, she was putting water on to boil.

"Do you want an omelette? Or something lighter, like cheese and crackers? Or there's a pork chop left over from dinner. I can heat it in the microwave."

Jeff took a deep breath. It was tempting to ask for an omelette because she would stay longer. But that wouldn't be fair. So he'd be honest. "The pork chop would be fine, but I can heat it up. Go on to bed."

She ignored him. Popping the pork chop into the microwave, she then added the leftover mashed potatoes. She made the instant coffee while they warmed. In minutes, Jeff had a warm snack ready for him.

Watching her was soothing. Like a sign that all was fine with the world, a thought hard to sustain after having an innocent child die. There had been nothing he could do. Not only did he have to treat the driver, but he also had to tell him that his careless driving had caused him to lose his child.

To his surprise, Diane took a seat beside him with her own cup of coffee. "Want to talk about it?"

His head jerked up. His wife had never wanted to hear about his work. She told him it was too depressing. He stared at Diane, tempted, but he refused to indulge himself. "No, but thanks for asking. It wouldn't be pleasant."

"I figured it must've been serious, you were gone so long."

"Yeah." He took a sip of coffee and sighed.

"Did everyone make it?"

He gulped. If he opened his mouth, he knew he'd spew out words describing the misery of the past few hours.

Diane stretched out her hand and touched his as it rested on the table. "Jeff? What happened?"

He couldn't resist such sweet concern. "A—a child died. Her father hadn't buckled her in. She flew out of the car and— There wasn't anything I could do." His voice was raw with the agony—and anger. "All he had to do was fasten a seat belt! But he'd had a few drinks. When I had to tell him she was dead, all he could say was his wife was going to kill him! It was like he'd lost a toy. No thought for the precious life he'd destroyed!"

As he'd feared, his anger had risen as he'd talked, until in the end, he was shouting. Diane clasped his hand with hers and leaned closer. "How old was she?"

"About three. A little older than Janie. The wife was working as a waitress at night to help pay the bills. He was supposed to stay home with his daughter, but he wanted to go out with the guys."

"And he took the baby?" Diane asked, sharing his anger.

"Yeah, it's senseless and selfish."

"How do you bear it, Jeff?" Diane asked.

Hearing sadness in her voice, Jeff felt guilty for upsetting her because of his own selfishness, so to comfort her, he released her hand and pulled her against him. "I shouldn't have said anything," he said, apology in his voice.

"I asked," Diane said simply, relaxing against him.

Her warmth soothed him. "Yeah, but I should have been strong enough to send you to bed without spoiling your evening."

"I wanted to know."

He knew that was true, but after his wife's behavior, he hadn't expected that reaction. Maybe that explained his weakness.

"Do you ever get used to it?" she whispered, her head on his shoulder.

"Yes, I did, and it frightened me. I saw too much. And I had no one to talk to about it, so I began to bury my feelings. I couldn't live with them inside me."

"Was that before you married?"

He tried to keep his voice even. "No. My wife didn't want to know about my work."

She didn't respond at once. He wondered if she'd dozed off, but then she spoke.

"Did she tell you about her day?"

"Yeah, but after a while, she didn't talk to me. She said she had friends at work who were more interested."

"A man?" she asked softly.

It was his turn to pause. He'd had suspicions and had resolved to question his wife. Then the accident that had killed her had happened. He'd never admitted those thoughts aloud before.

"Maybe," he finally muttered.

She sighed. "I always thought the good thing about marriage was having someone to share the good things and the bad. Now you're telling me even that doesn't work."

"Maybe we didn't work hard enough. Or maybe we were wrong for each other."

He wanted to say more to point out that he felt closer to Diane than he ever had his wife. That maybe he'd been moved by hormones more than having things in common.

"Maybe so. There was this guy…I thought I loved him. Then he told me there was no need to stay in school, unless I wanted to take gourmet cooking lessons. After all, I'd be staying home with the children."

Jeff hugged her close and murmured, "He was an idiot!" And Jeff considered himself lucky that she'd sent the jerk on his way. Except he'd told himself that they had different goals which made them wrong for each other. And he was too old for Diane—but he kept forgetting that fact.

He forgot it so totally now that he found himself nibbling on her soft mouth, wanting to be closer to her, wanting her to know how grateful he was for her listening, for being there for him.

Instead of protesting, Diane encouraged him, opening to him.

Then Jeff really forgot.

Chapter Thirteen

Diane lost herself in Jeff's arms. The emotions he'd evoked, not only by the night's events, but also by what he'd revealed about his marriage, made her want to comfort and console. But there was more, a bonding intensified by the spark that burst into flames if she didn't run away at once.

Tonight she hadn't run at all.

He lifted her from her chair into his lap, and she felt surrounded by his warmth. His hands molded her breasts. His lips devoured her lips, then nibbled on her neck, going lower each time.

When he reached for the hem of her T-shirt and began to raise it, she realized she had to call a halt before it was too late. He didn't love her. Relief was what he was seeking. Relief from the horrors of the night. From the loneliness she'd heard in his voice.

Wrenching her mouth from his delicious hold, she buried her face against his neck. "Jeff!" Her husky protest sounded like a plea for more rather than an order to halt.

Maybe because she was enjoying herself too much.

His hands were on her midriff, warming her skin as they slowly inched her T-shirt up to her breasts, and Diane realized they were swiftly approaching the point where she'd throw common sense out the door.

More insistently, she tried again. "Jeff, we have to stop. We can't—we're not—"

It was difficult to think coherently, even when Jeff's hands stilled. The urge to beg him to ignore her conscience was strong, but she clung to the thought that sleeping with Jeff would be wrong. Delightfully wrong.

"Are you sure? We're both free...and we want each other," he muttered. Slowly, his hands pulled back from touching her.

She should've immediately told him she was sure. He was a gentleman. He was leaving the choice up to her. Wasn't that what she wanted? To determine her own future? To make her own choices? So what did she want?

"Yes, I'm sure," she whispered. Her heart soared as she noted his disappointment. "I'm sure I want you," she added.

He froze, as if he couldn't believe her words. Then his hands, his wonderful hands, returned to her skin. Shivers went through her and her heart raced as she sank against his body.

"Sweetheart, let's go...to the sofa," he urged, opting for the closest place.

Together they moved to the den, dropping clothing on the way. Jeff lowered her to the cushions and then joined her.

The strength of their desire urged them both on, but Jeff's tenderness added a sweetness Diane hadn't expected. Jeff had her senses *and* her heart. When they both exploded in satisfaction, Diane felt her world had changed...all for the better.

WHEN THE MORNING CAME, cold reason came with it. Jeff realized their lovemaking may have been— was—extraordinary, but it was also a momentary thing. Diane didn't want to stay in Cactus. And Jeff didn't want to leave. Any more such intimacy as last night and he would suffer—greatly.

Jeff knew he had to do something to ensure they didn't make love again. Hopefully he wouldn't have any more emergency calls until after his guests vacated his house.

He winced. Just thinking about their departure created an ache. Paul and the children were enjoyable and gave him a sense of family he'd never experienced before. Diane...he didn't have words to describe what Diane added to his life.

But it was important that he remembered it was temporary. And any more late night sharing with Diane might mean he'd forget that important fact.

He didn't enjoy a leisurely breakfast the next morning. Samantha usually covered the morning office hours because he took the emergency calls at night. He'd really enjoyed sharing the first meal of the day with Diane.

So he chose to grab a cup of coffee and make a biscuit sandwich with sausage and scrambled eggs. "Sorry, I need to get into the office early. I need to talk to Cal this morning about the accident last night."

"Oh. Okay. Here's a napkin," Diane said, not fussing about his change of routine. "Ask him what he's found out about Mrs. Duncan's accident, too."

"Yeah, sure. Are you bringing Toby to see his mother?"

"Yes, of course. I think I'll try taking Janie again today."

He couldn't completely withdraw. "Let me know when you're coming in and I'll meet you. In case you need me."

"I hate to interrupt your day. I'm sure we'll be fine."

But I won't. "Uh, like I said, just in case." He was congratulating himself on how well he'd resisted her until he almost bent down and brushed her lips with his.

The hunger that seized him, that encouraged him to sweep her into his arms, wiped away that self-praise. He rushed out of the house without touching her.

DIANE STARED after Jeff, wondering why he'd backed away. He certainly hadn't done so last night. Maybe he'd changed his mind about her. Maybe he was afraid she'd expect more than he was willing to give. She should have told him she wasn't expecting him to commit to her. Did she?

She hadn't meant to scare him out of breakfast. A man needed good food to start his day.

The children came to the kitchen. "Where's Dr. Jeff?" Toby asked, looking around as he climbed into the chair he used.

"He's already gone to work, sweetie," Diane told him as she helped Janie into her chair. "Ready for breakfast?"

Later, with the dishes done, she dressed the children to go to the hospital. Toby had seen his mother several times and seemed to take the visits in stride, now. Janie, however, was a different matter. Diane hoped she'd finally understand that her mother was getting better all the time and would soon be with her again. Right now, Mrs. Duncan was doing some physical therapy as well as building her strength.

"Will we see Dr. Jeff?" Toby asked as she led them out to the car.

"I don't know. I called to let him know we were coming, but he's busy right now. I'm sure he'll come if he can. We can see your mom even if he can't come by, okay?"

She'd been hesitant about calling Jeff anyway, but he'd been so insistent.

After leaving a note for Hannah, telling her where they were, she got the children in the car and drove the two blocks to the hospital.

JEFF HAD DECIDED that midmorning was a good time to stop by Cal's office. He'd wanted to discuss the recent car accident with the sheriff. But he discovered that Cal was currently occupied and so sat down to wait to see the lawman.

He stood when he heard Cal's voice. "Sorry, Mr. Andheim, that it took so long, but some of my men were city cops, not farmers. They handle bad guys better than they do runaway pigs."

"I know, Sheriff, but I do appreciate the help. As soon as I sign the paperwork, I'll be out of your hair."

"I appreciate your cooperation," Cal said with a nod. Then he spotted Jeff in his office.

"Mornin', Jeff. You're here about that wreck last night?"

"I thought I'd check in. You know the child died? Are you going to charge the man with manslaughter?"

Cal's face turned grim. "Yeah. It'll be up to the judge if he serves any time. But if he doesn't, maybe being charged will scare him."

"Do you need any information from me about last night?"

Cal frowned. "Did the child die immediately? Did the man neglect to render aid?"

Jeff sighed. "No. Unfortunately, the little girl couldn't be helped by anyone."

Cal nodded. "I figured."

"Diane wanted to know if you've gotten any more information on Evie Duncan's accident."

"Not much. I'd guess the car that hit them was sold immediately. I've had my deputies visit the car dealers in Lubbock and any of the small towns around here, but no luck."

"Okay, I'll—"

"Good morning, son. Oh, Jeff, I didn't know you were here," Mabel Baxter said as she entered Cal's office. "Do I need to wait outside?"

"Not on my account, Mabel," Jeff said to Cal's mother, one of the original matchmakers in Cactus.

Cal groaned and shook his head. "Don't encourage her, Jeff. She forgets she's talking to the sheriff of this county."

She rolled her eyes. "Since your father was sheriff before you, I think I can figure it out. I just had a question about the festival."

"I'll get out of here, then," Jeff said.

"Oh, no, I have a question for you, too," Mabel said, waving him back into his chair.

Jeff sat down, apprehension flowing through him. "Okay."

"Everything is going well, but I need to know if there are any areas off-limits to the booths." That question was clearly addressed to Cal, so Jeff sat quietly as he and his mother discussed particulars.

When she'd finished with Cal, she turned to Jeff. "We've had a lot of volunteers for the kissing booth, Jeff. Does it matter if someone replaces you? You'll be giving shots and I don't think you should have to work the entire time."

Jeff sighed with relief. "I don't mind at all, Mabel."

"Well, I didn't know since Diane was working it, but—"

"She's not!" Jeff exclaimed. He'd forgotten to notify the organizers about that change. He explained about the arrangements he'd made.

"Oh, I'm glad I talked to you," Mabel agreed. Just then, a deep male voice near the desk of Betty, Cal's receptionist, drew their attentions. "Can you give me directions to the Peters's home?"

"Who you looking for, hon?" Betty asked.

Jeff frowned and stood, moving toward the man without thinking. He noticed that the man was dressed in a designer suit with a silk tie, and that he was eight or ten years younger than him.

The man frowned, apparently not caring for the intrusive question.

"I don't think that's any of your business," he replied stiffly, glaring at Betty.

Betty looked down her nose at him, apparently not intimidated by his displeasure. "Then I guess I can't help you."

He opened his mouth, presumably to give her a piece of his mind, but Cal interrupted.

"May I help you?" the sheriff asked coolly.

"I was asking for directions, but apparently you demand a third degree before I get an answer and I find that ridiculous!"

"Maybe you'll understand when I tell you that the Peters's home caught fire and the family are temporarily living in different places rather than together. Or, if you prefer, we can send you on a useless drive to what's left of the house.''

Though his cheeks flushed, the man offered no apology. "Very well. I need to find Diane."

"Maybe if you apologize to Betty and ask again, you'll get the information you need," Cal suggested as he turned back to his office.

Jeff wasn't about to leave. He wanted to know who the man was and what business he had with Diane.

Mabel appeared to have the same interest.

Instead of following Cal's suggestion, the man turned to Betty and snapped, "Where is she?"

Cal proved he was still listening when he spun around and retraced his steps.

Betty said nothing, a smile on her lips. She knew her boss well.

Cal eyed the man and said, "Apparently you didn't hear my instructions, Mr...? I believe I told you to apologize before you asked your question. And if I were you, I'd be a lot more civil about it, too."

Jeff smiled. Cal might be older than the young man, but the steel in his voice would've convinced Jeff to follow his orders.

The man muttered something under his breath, but Cal stood there staring at him, his hands on his hips.

Finally, the man faced Betty. "My apologies. I'd appreciate your giving me Diane Peters's location."

His voice was stiff and unfriendly, unlike most people in Cactus, but the words were appropriate.

Betty looked at Jeff. "Doctor?"

Reluctantly, Jeff responded to her prompting. "Diane and her brother Paul are staying at my house until the end of the month."

"That's very generous of you and your wife. I'll try to take Diane off your hands." This time he offered a smile, but it didn't charm Jeff. Nor did his words.

"Not necessary. I have plenty of room."

"Are you a friend of Diane's from Lubbock?" Mabel asked, speaking for the first time.

Though the man raised one eyebrow, seeming to silently question why she was asking, a quick glance at Cal had him shifting his gaze back to Mabel. "I'm more than a friend. I'm her fiancé."

WHEN DIANE REACHED the small hospital, she grabbed the children's hands and led them inside. By now, Toby knew the route and if she didn't hold him back, he'd burst into his mother's room without warning.

"Where's Dr. Jeff?" Toby asked as soon as he got inside. "I want to ask him if he'll play cars with me again."

"I'm sure he will. But Paul will be back this afternoon, so if Dr. Jeff can't, maybe he'll play with you," Diane assured him, but she, too, looked around for Jeff.

For Toby's sake, of course, she told herself.

"Mama?" Janie asked, suddenly connecting the hospital with her mother.

"Yes, Janie, we're going to see your mama. She's doing much better." She picked up Janie and cuddled her against herself, hoping to keep the little girl calm.

One of the nurses came out of Evie Duncan's room, which was no longer isolated.

Diane called out to her. "Is Dr. Jeff around?"

"Haven't seen him, but I'll check his office. You visiting Mrs. Duncan?"

"Yes, we are. Can you let Dr. Jeff know we're here if you find him?"

"Sure will."

Diane took the children into the room and let them greet their mother. Then she settled in a nearby chair, sitting Janie on the bed and allowing Toby to stand next to her.

She'd made it a point to relieve Evie's worries about the well-being of her children and her financial situation, and they talked like old friends now. Florence had visited the afternoon before, giving Evie information about the progress of the festival again. She relayed what she knew to Diane.

"I had no idea they'd already done so much," Diane exclaimed.

"Florence said you had your hands full with my kids. I hope they're not too much for you."

Diane smiled. "There were six of us, Evie, and Jeff just hired a housekeeper since I'm working the afternoons now, so there's no problem."

"Everyone here is so nice!" Evie exclaimed with a sigh. "I feel like I should be doing something."

"You are doing something. You're making a great recovery," Diane assured her. "Jeff says you're a strong woman."

"I had no choice since my husband died," Evie said quietly, stroking Janie's hair while she held Toby's hand.

Diane thought of her own mother. "No, you had a choice. But you chose the right one, even if it is hard. My mother fell to pieces in the same situation. It was my sister who took care of us."

Evie stared at her. "Don't blame your mother, Diane. I'm sure she did the best she could."

Diane blinked away the tears. "I know," she whispered. "Anyway, back to the festival. We hope it will bring in enough money to pay your medical bills and help you get a new start." She smiled encouragingly.

Tears filled Evie's eyes. "That's so incredible. I don't know how to thank all of you."

"Cal, our sheriff," Diane continued, "is still trying to find out who hit you. If he can, maybe their insurance will pay for your car, too. I asked Jeff to ask him how the investigation was going. He had to see him this morning on another matter. I guess that's where he is."

Toby beamed. "Me and Dr. Jeff played cars."

"Dr. Jeff and I," Evie gently corrected.

"Yeah," Toby agreed, still smiling.

"Baby!" Janie exclaimed and looked around her.

"Baby's at home, sweetie," Diane reminded her. "But you showed Mama your baby last time you came." When she looked at Evie she saw her blank face. "Doll," she mouthed.

"Oh, yes, your baby," Evie nodded. Then she frowned at Diane. "She didn't have a baby. Where—"

Diane smiled. "We bought her baby and Toby's cars so they'd have something to play with to—to cheer them up."

"I—I think I had some money in my purse. But I don't know where it is. If you'll ask someone—"

"That's not necessary, Evie. They didn't cost much and your children are so sweet. You must be a great parent."

Evie wiped the tears from her eyes. "Cactus is—is so incredible. The people here are—"

She couldn't seem to come up with other superlatives.

Diane smiled again. "You know, maybe you should think about staying here. If you don't have family in Lubbock, this place is wonderful for raising children. Especially as a single parent. Everyone knows everyone else and helps keep an eye out for problems."

"Is that why you're here?"

Diane blinked several times, thinking about her plans to leave Cactus. She believed what she'd said. Cactus *was* a wonderful place to raise children. But she'd decided not to have children. And still wasn't, she sharply reminded herself.

"I'm here because I was born and raised here. My family's still here. I love it here." Somehow, she didn't see a need to mention her future plans.

"You said you have a large family. You're lucky."

"Yes, I am."

"Mama, when are you coming home?" Toby asked, tired of all the chatter.

Evie looked troubled. "I don't know, baby. The doctor said he hoped I could go to the festival they're having. But I won't be able to go back to work that soon. I hadn't thought about the apartment. I probably need to send in rent for July soon."

"I'll talk to Cal about it. He'll bring you your purse, if you want it. And I'll discuss your apartment with him. Maybe we can store your stuff and save you some money."

"I'll need somewhere to live while I'm recovering. But I don't know if I'll have enough money to pay for it until I go back to work. Oh, Diane, what am I going to do?"

Diane regretted her chat with Evie since it only brought more worry to her.

The phone beside the bed rang. "Want me to answer it for you?" Diane asked.

Evie nodded.

"Hello?"

The caller didn't identify himself, but Diane recognized his voice. However, it didn't have the lazy charm she usually heard. "Diane?"

"Yes, Jeff. Where are you?"

"In Cal's office. Can you come over here at once?"

There was a sharp bite to his words that surprised her. "What's wrong?"

"Your fiancé's here." And he hung up.

Chapter Fourteen

Jeff hung up the phone, keeping his back to the others. But he heard Mabel asking a question that should have occurred to him. But he'd been too upset to think.

"I hadn't heard Diane was engaged. When did you two get together?"

Jeff spun around to stare at the man as he waited for the answer.

"Well," the well-dressed man said, giving Mabel a shy smile that Jeff decided at once was a fake. "We're not actually engaged at the moment, but we once were. I've come to win her back."

His confidence grated on Jeff's nerves. Though Jeff knew he wasn't what Diane wanted, surely she could do better than this—this preppy jerk!

"Oh, my!" Mabel exclaimed, a beaming smile on her face. "How romantic!"

Jeff wanted to hit something…or someone.

Cal stepped forward. "I'm Cal Baxter. I don't believe you gave your name."

"Thomas Westerby."

After he shook Cal's hand, Thomas stuck out his hand toward Jeff.

Jeff didn't want to shake hands with the man who intended to take Diane out of his life. But he had no choice. "Dr. Jeff Hausen," he muttered.

"So you'll be staying a few days?" Mabel asked.

Jeff frowned. Something was going on. He sensed a purpose in Mabel's words that had him worried. Did she think she could take credit for this romance?

"Yes, I'm going to visit and get to know Di's family," Thomas assured her with easy confidence.

"That's a problem," Mabel said, frowning.

"Why?" Thomas snapped, all the charm gone from his voice. He clearly didn't like his plans challenged.

"Well, with the house burned, her parents are staying with her sister, Katie. They don't have room for guests. And Diane and Paul and the children are staying with— Jeff!" she exclaimed, spinning around. "You have an empty bedroom!"

It was the first time Jeff had ever had the urge to choke a person. He'd never wanted the assistance of the matchmakers. He certainly didn't want them to help Diane leave Cactus.

But he wanted Diane to be happy. She wanted a big city, sophistication. That wasn't him. Maybe she could talk this Thomas into no children.

And *he* wouldn't lose control anymore, like he had last night.

"Sure, I have an empty bedroom. You're welcome to stay if Diane— I mean, shouldn't you talk to Diane first?''

"Oh, we'll talk, but I can assure you we'll be engaged in no time. Thanks, Dr. Hausen.''

Jeff felt like a part of him had died. All along he'd told himself Diane wasn't for him, but his heart had refused to believe it. Now he had no choice.

"Diane!" Thomas Westerby exclaimed suddenly, as she entered the sheriff's office. There was a big smile on the man's face as he spread his arms open wide.

"Hello, Tom," she said, no emotion in her voice. "Excuse me. I need to talk to Cal and Jeff... privately.''

Cal frowned. "Is something wrong?''

"What is it?" Jeff asked at the same time.

"You can talk to them later," Westerby insisted. "We have more important things to discuss.''

She ignored him, walking around him toward Cal's office.

Jeff turned to follow her, his heart lifting.

"Diane, you don't understand. I've forgiven you!" Thomas exclaimed, moving after her.

"I'm busy, Tom." She walked into Cal's office.

Over his shoulder, as he followed Diane, Jeff saw Cal close the door behind him.

As if the man's appearance meant nothing to her, Diane said at once, "It's Evie.''

Jeff stepped closer, wanting to touch her but holding back. "What about Evie?''

"I upset her. We were talking, and I told her she

should think about staying in Cactus because it's a good place for raising children. Suddenly she realized she needed to pay rent for July, but she's not sure she'll be able to go to work that soon, and if she can't, she won't have money for the next month. I said maybe we could store her stuff and save her money, but she got all upset.''

"Hmm, I hadn't thought of that," Cal said, rubbing his chin.

"I'll go talk to her," Jeff volunteered. He wanted to make sure Evie stayed relaxed and improving.

"She needs her purse," Diane added. "Do you have it, Cal?"

"Yeah. Why does she need it?"

Diane looked disgusted. "A woman feels lost without her purse, that's why!"

Cal grinned. "Yeah, I should've thought of that. Okay, I'll take her her purse."

They smiled at each other, and Jeff felt excluded. Or maybe it was because he was upset about Thomas Westerby. But there was no time to talk. Cal had his hand on the doorknob.

He paused, "Uh, Diane, I'm sorry about what my mom did." Then he opened the door.

DIANE PAUSED IN THE open door, watching Cal and Jeff leave the building. She hadn't had a lot of enthusiasm for visiting with Thomas Westerby, though she'd easily guessed who had arrived by Jeff's telephone message. But now she warily stared at the other two waiting for her.

What had Cal meant?

Mabel stepped forward. "Diane, isn't it exciting to see Thomas again? I mean, I shouldn't spoil his surprise, should I? But Jeff agreed he could stay in the spare bedroom at his house so you two can visit. Wasn't that sweet of him?"

"Oh, yes, sweet," Diane muttered. Now she knew what Cal meant. But what had Jeff had in mind? Did he want her to marry someone and get out of his hair? Did he want to avoid any more circumstances like last night? He'd certainly tried to avoid her this morning.

Diane's cheeks flushed, concluding her reasoning was right. He thought she was chasing him. Well, she didn't need to endure Thomas Westerby in the same house to understand. She'd get rid of him right away.

"But I doubt that will be necessary," she added firmly. "Tom and I have nothing to talk about."

"Now that's where you're wrong, Di, honey," Thomas intervened, his voice enthusiastic. "I've changed. We want the same things. Come on, let's go find somewhere private to talk," he said, reaching out for her hand.

She stepped back. "I don't mind talking in front of Mabel."

"And me," Betty reminded her.

"I insist!" Thomas said, irritation on his face.

So he thought he could waltz in and convince her to take up where they left off four years ago? Typical. But he wasn't going to leave until they had their little talk.

"All right, but I have to go to work in an hour. You can buy me lunch."

"Of course, I'd be delighted."

"Where are the children?" Mabel suddenly asked.

"I called Paul and he met me at the hospital. He'll take care of them until Hannah gets to Jeff's house."

"Oh, good. I'll let you two lovebirds go to lunch, then." She winked at Diane, then left.

"Is there a decent restaurant in this slug of a town?" Thomas asked, a sneer in his voice.

Betty glared at him, but Diane wasn't surprised. "I think there's one that will be expensive enough. Come on."

She walked fast across the town square. When she reached the front steps of The Last Roundup, she paused and said, "By the way, I wouldn't criticize the restaurant. The sheriff's wife owns it."

Tom looked startled and not a little apprehensive.

Good. She didn't intend to make his visit pleasant.

After they were shown to a booth, he looked around, relieved. "This doesn't seem so bad."

Diane rolled her eyes and picked up the menu. She knew it by memory, of course, but it served as an excuse to avoid conversation. She carefully selected the most expensive steak on the menu.

After they'd given their order to the waitress, she had no more excuses. "Why are you here, Tom?"

"I prefer Thomas now," he pointed out, looking down his nose at her.

"I don't care what you prefer. Why are you here?"

She saw him struggle to control his irritation at her cavalier dismissal of his request. Finally, he smiled, his attitude quite superior.

"I'm here to admit I was wrong."

She took a sip of water. "Well, if that's all, I really need to go." Sliding over to the edge of the booth, she was prepared to leave, but he grabbed her wrist.

"I'm trying to apologize!" he snapped.

"For what?"

"For breaking up with you. I made a mistake. I thought you were wrong when you said you didn't want children."

When she didn't say anything, he apparently took her silence as encouragement. "I think a young professional couple is much better. We can say we'll have children one day. By the time they realize we're not having children, my bosses won't be able to dismiss me because I'll be too valuable." He sat back against the booth and beamed at her.

Fortunately, the waitress arrived with their food, which gave Diane time to think about her response. She began eating as soon as the waitress left.

"Diane! You haven't said anything."

"This steak is really good," she pointed out.

"I'm telling you we can get married now!" he snapped.

"No, thank you." The pompous jerk!

"Didn't you understand?"

"Yes. You'd better eat your steak before it gets cold."

He stared at her, then picked up his knife and fork. "I get it," he said before he cut his steak and took a bite.

She didn't answer.

"You want your pound of flesh because I dumped you."

"If I remember correctly, I dumped you." Thank goodness. The man was an absolute egocentric idiot.

"Because I wanted to have a family. A normal request." When she said nothing, he said, "Don't worry, I'm patient. I know you're stubborn, but I'll be able to persuade you after a couple of days. And since the doctor has invited me to stay, no problem." With a look of superior satisfaction, he ate his steak.

She wasn't going to be able to get away from this jerk, Diane thought. Jeff must feel the same way about her.

The next few days were going to be difficult.

"HANNAH?" JEFF SAID TO the woman on the other end of the phone. "I called to tell you I asked someone to stay with us for a couple of days. I hope you don't mind."

"Do you mean Mr. Westerby?"

Jeff clutched the telephone more tightly. "Yeah. Is he there?" He'd hoped the man would refuse his offer. He'd prayed Westerby would leave town. He'd admitted it would probably be better if he did and took Diane with him.

But Jeff didn't want her to go.

"I've met him. Diane told me not to do things for him. Is that right?"

"What do you mean?"

"Well, he asked me to make the bed in his room, but Diane gave me strict instructions he was to do his own bed. So I told him I couldn't leave the children."

Jeff heard her concern. "You did fine. He's Diane's guest, so do whatever she says. Is everything else all right? Did Diane go to work?"

"Oh, yes. She left early."

"Good. Thanks. If you need anything, just call me."

"I will. Especially if that man is mean to the kids again."

Jeff hung up the phone and stared across his office. What a mess! He wouldn't change the past couple of weeks, having the Peters' and the children in his life. But he didn't want Thomas Westerby there.

One of his nurses knocked on his office door, letting him know that his next patient was ready. His last patient. It was only four o'clock, but he decided to go home after he'd seen his patient. The children needed him.

DIANE'S AFTERNOON HAD become very busy. The case she'd been assigned to was an interesting one, and she got wrapped up in the details and the possible defense. But she did call home, midway through the afternoon. As she'd expected, Thomas had tried to convince Hannah to make up his bed for him. But he hadn't bothered the children, and that was the most important thing.

Suddenly, she lifted the receiver and called a number in Lubbock. Sherry Wilson had been a suitemate in undergrad. When she answered the phone, Diane explained why she was calling.

"Can you tell me what Tom's been up to these past years?"

"Tom Westerby? The one you used to date? No, I can't say I can. I haven't seen him in a while. Need me to find out?"

"Yeah, Sherry, if you don't mind. I know it will take some time, but—"

"No problem. You know I love gossip. I'll try to call you back tomorrow. What number do I use?"

After she hung up the phone, Diane wandered downstairs to tell Alexandra that she'd made a personal call and she would pay for it as soon as the bill came in.

"Don't worry about it, Di, as long as it's not a habit. We all have moments when we need to make a call."

"Thanks, Alex. You know, I've heard about people working in the big law firms. They're under so much pressure. I think I like working here better."

"You beginning to change your mind about the

big city?'' Alex asked with a smile. ''Because if you are, we'll all be pleased.''

''Really? You're not just saying that because Gabe is my brother-in-law?'' Diane had wondered about the one year job they'd given her. She figured Gabe had arranged it.

''No way. Your credentials are impressive. And Gabe was very pleased with what you found in one day. When you finish up that case, I'd love some help, too.''

Diane chuckled. ''Sure thing. You know, I haven't quite decided what I'm going to do.''

''But if you marry that Westerby man, you won't be here, will you?''

Diane's head snapped up and she stared at Alexandra. ''How do you know about that?''

''Come on, Di, we're in Cactus. Gossip central. Mabel was there for the encounter, remember? When any of those ladies get a sniff of matrimony, they go on red alert.'' Alexandra leaned back in her chair. ''You know how they are.''

''Well, they can just forget it. Tom is a jerk, and I want nothing to do with him.''

''Good. That means there's a chance you're staying.''

BY THE TIME DIANE HAD gotten home for dinner, Hannah was putting everything on the table. ''Hi, need some help?''

''No, it's almost ready. Uh, you want to go to the

den and join Mr. Westerby and Dr. Jeff? They've been chatting for a while.''

"No, I don't. Is everything all right?''

Hannah shrugged her shoulders and kept her attention on the mashed potatoes she was putting in a bowl.

Diane couldn't imagine Jeff was enjoying himself. But he'd invited the man to stay, so it was only right that he had to entertain him. "Uh, Hannah, I'm going to change the seating order at the table. I want you to sit at the end where I usually sit. I'll put Toby next to you, then Janie, then me, next to Jeff. Paul can sit with Tom on the other side of the table. I don't want either of the children to sit by him.''

"Good thinking.''

"Where are the children?''

"They're upstairs with Paul. He didn't get along with Mr. Starchy Pants either.'' Then she gasped and covered her mouth with her hand. "Sorry, I didn't mean—''

"Don't worry about it. It sounds pretty accurate to me. I'll go help the kids wash up and explain the change in seating. Can you put another chair on this side?''

At Hannah's nod, Diane ran up the stairs.

Chapter Fifteen

Jeff left early again the next morning. But not because of Diane. Well, not exactly. But he definitely couldn't stand the idea of facing Thomas Westerby. Not after dinner last night.

He'd never met a more pompous, conceited man. The thought of Diane giving her life to this undeserving man drove him crazy. Or maybe it was jealousy he was feeling. But he'd go crazy if he had to watch the man try to sway Diane.

He stopped by Cal's office to see what he'd decided about Evie's apartment. He'd tried to convince her yesterday to relax and not worry about anything. With limited success. Cal had promised to check everything out and get back to her.

"Is Cal in?" Jeff asked Betty.

Cal stuck his head out of the office. "I was about to go to The Lemon Drop Shop for breakfast. Want to join me?"

Jeff drew a breath of anticipation. "Yeah, I haven't had breakfast yet."

"You being ignored in your own house?"

Jeff grinned. "Nope. I just couldn't stand another minute with Mr. Thomas Westerby. I owe your mother some grief for her idea."

Cal shook his head. "Yeah. I talked to her about it yesterday."

"What was she thinking?" Jeff exclaimed as they walked across the square.

"You don't want to know," Cal said, not looking at him.

Jeff came to an abrupt halt. "Wait a minute. You mean she actually has a plan? She wants Diane to marry that man?"

Cal took his arm and pulled him along to the shop. Once they'd gotten sausage rolls and coffee and sat down outside, he said, "She doesn't want Diane to marry the man."

"Neither do I!" Jeff exclaimed. Then he ducked his head and added, "I want her to be happy, though."

"Yeah. Here comes Spence and Gabe."

Jeff looked up to see the two friends walking toward them. "Were you expecting them?"

"Yeah, didn't you get my message?" Cal asked, staring at him.

"What message? I stopped by on the way to my office."

"Oh. Well, I left you a message at the office to meet us here to decide how to handle Evie's problems."

"Good thing I came, then," Jeff said, scooting his chair over to make room for the other two.

Soon the four men had come to an agreement. They were going to take Spence and Tuck's trucks into Lubbock that evening and load up Evie's belongings. Tuck couldn't go because of a prior commitment, and Mac was putting in long hours on a legal problem, but they figured the four of them could manage.

"Melanie's coming, too. Mom's going to take the kids and keep them overnight," Spence added with a grin. "A one-night second honeymoon."

"Hey, I'll see if Jess wants to come, too," Cal said. "Mom owes us some baby-sitting after what she did to Jeff."

"Wait a minute. How does her baby-sitting for you help me out?" Jeff asked. "She should—never mind." Mabel taking care of Toby and Janie wouldn't help him because Westerby would still be around.

Besides, he wasn't going to ever have a honeymoon with Diane.

THE MORNING WAS STRESSFUL for Diane. Paul had avoided Tom all the evening before, leaving Diane to entertain their guest. He'd kept trying to convince her to discuss their relationship, but she hadn't wanted to continue the conversation. Jeff had retreated to his room directly after dinner and had left early this morning. So Diane hadn't been able to explain her concerns about Tom to Jeff. She wanted their houseguest gone, fast.

"Paul, you will be home this evening, won't you?" she asked as she served breakfast to him and the children. Tom had not yet awakened.

"Why?" he asked, a suspicious look on his face.

"Because I need help keeping the kids away from Tom."

"I don't care if they upset him."

"That's not a problem for me, either," she explained, "but he makes Toby feel bad. Even Janie gets upset. She doesn't like him."

"She's not alone," Paul muttered.

"Hopefully, I'll have convinced him to leave before then, but I need you here. Jeff's tired when he comes in."

"Yeah, he's a good guy. He sure doesn't deserve ol' Tom droning on and on about all his accomplishments."

"So you'll be here?"

Paul grimaced. "Okay, okay, but I won't like it!"

"Me, neither."

When Tom came downstairs at eleven, he asked for breakfast.

"We ate earlier, Tom. You can make yourself some toast if you want. It's not long until lunch," Diane said. She'd had a peaceful morning. Now, Paul and the children were sneaking into the den to watch a video. She was in the middle of baking more cookies and couldn't escape.

"Have you been thinking about my proposal, Di?

With both of us working, we'll have an excellent portfolio in no time.''

"How romantic," she said, keeping her back to him.

When his arms came around her, she was repulsed. The nausea that filled her propelled her elbows backward even harder.

"Oouf! Hey!" Tom complained.

"Sorry, but I don't like being crowded." She broke two eggs into the cookie mixture, wishing she could smash them on Tom's nose.

How could she ever have thought she would marry this man? She'd thought she was being focused on a law career. But why had she shut out so completely things she enjoyed?

"Come on, baby. We'll be great together. We always were in bed," Tom said. But Diane *hadn't* enjoyed the sex. She'd wondered why some women seemed willing to do anything for sexual pleasure.

When she met Jeff, when she spent time in his arms, she discovered a sexual hunger that was hard to resist. Explosive. She'd never found that with Tom.

Frowning, distracted by what she'd discovered about herself, she said, "Go away, Tom. I'm not going to marry you." Her voice was flat. His reaction didn't matter to her.

"You'll change your mind when I take you in my arms," Tom said, but she noticed that he rubbed his ribs and didn't come any closer.

"No, I won't."

"Hello?" Hannah called as she let herself in the back door.

"Come in, Hannah," Diane called with relief.

The smile on the housekeeper's face faded as she realized Thomas Westerby was in the kitchen with Diane. "Good morning, Mr. Westerby," she said politely.

Tom nodded at her, then turned back to Diane. "May I speak to you privately, Diane?"

"No." She didn't coat her response with politeness.

"I'm not leaving. Tonight I'll show you why you should marry me. I know you. Just wait." Then he turned and stomped out of the kitchen.

Diane stared after him.

AS SOON AS DIANE GOT to the office after lunch, she knocked on Gabe's door.

"Oh, hi, Di. That case you found yesterday with almost the same situation was great. Thanks."

"I'm glad it helped. Uh, is Katie at home or the shop today?"

Gabe lifted his head and stared at Diane. "She's home. Why? Is anything wrong?"

"I just need to talk to her."

"You're okay with Jeff going with us tonight, then?"

Diane froze. She'd scarcely spoken to Jeff since Tom arrived yesterday morning. "What are you talking about?"

"A bunch of us are driving to Lubbock to pick

up Evie and the children's belonging. We won't be back until late."

She closed her eyes. Jeff was definitely avoiding her. He'd slipped out early this morning, before she'd gotten to the kitchen. She'd thought it was a medical emergency.

Instead, he was avoiding her again.

"Diane?"

She snapped her eyes open to find Gabe coming toward her, concern on his face.

"I'm fine. I'm going to call Katie," she told him as she backed out of his office. "That's all. I need to talk to Katie."

"Okay," he agreed. Diane wasn't surprised to see him reach for his phone as she walked away. She knew he'd call Katie and warn her something was up. They shared everything. They had a great marriage. The kind Diane now knew she wanted.

But it didn't appear Jeff was interested.

She gave Gabe five minutes before she called her sister's home.

Katie immediately offered to come to the law office, but Diane asked her to meet her in half an hour at the shop. She didn't want to talk at work.

Then she called Jeff. "Is Dr. Hausen in?"

"May I say who's calling?"

"Marybelle, it's Diane."

"Oh, I'll get him," the woman said and put down the phone.

Diane would like to think Jeff had left instructions to let him know if she called. But Marybelle's response was probably because Diane had known Marybelle since her own birth. The woman had worked for Doc for years. After a minute, Jeff answered. "Diane? Is anything wrong?"

"I didn't realize you'd be away tonight. I just wanted to see if you knew what time you'd be home. The kids will ask." That was the least pushy way she could discuss his plans. And the fact that he hadn't told her.

"Sorry, no, I don't know when I'll be home. Probably late. I didn't know until this morning, and I was going to call you, but I had an emergency and—"

"You don't have to check your schedule with me, Jeff. We're staying at your house, that's all," she said frostily. He'd made it sound like she was accusing him of something!

Well, of course, she was, but she knew she shouldn't.

"We're loading all of Evie's belongings," he said.

"I know. Well, I don't want to keep you."

"Wait! Are you—are you doing okay?"

Like she'd tell him her problems when he didn't even want to be around her. "Fine."

"Ah. I'll see you tomorrow, then."

She hung up the phone. Of course, he would. Unless he left early again. She wanted to ask him to retract his invitation to Tom. The man seemed determined to stalk her. And Jeff was helping him.

Because he wanted her gone.

A tear traced a path down her cheek, but she scrubbed it away. She may have figured out her problem too late, but at least it was in time to avoid someone like Thomas Westerby.

WHEN DIANE REACHED The Lemon Drop Shop, she found her sister in the kitchen waiting for her. The baking for the day was done, and the room was pristine and empty.

"Katie? I hope you don't mind—"

"You know I don't," Katie assured her, wrapping her in a close hug. "What's wrong?"

Before Diane could explain, Katie led her to a small table in the corner, where they could sit down.

"I need to ask you something."

"Okay. I'll even share my next recipe with you," Katie promised, smiling. She'd sold several recipes to the corporation that owned franchises of The Last Roundup, Jessica Baxter's restaurant.

"It's not—it's Mom."

Katie said nothing, but frowned and waited.

"Do you resent Mom?"

Katie did a double take, then shook her head no. "Why would I?"

"Oh, come on, Katie. You can't be that much of a saint. You gave up your life for all of us. Mom was too weak to help herself, much less us. You gave up Gabe, letting him think you didn't love him so he'd go to law school. Why wouldn't you resent her?"

Katie stared at her hands, probably thinking about

all the backbreaking work she'd done, the college degree she'd forsaken, the emotional drain of caring for her family.

Diane was surprised when she smiled.

"I'll confess to being irritated with her a few times, especially when she didn't deal with the day-to-day difficulties."

Relief flooded Diane. She'd begun to wonder if she was a monster.

"Are *you* upset with her?"

"No, with myself," Diane confessed. "I—I haven't spent much time with Mom. In fact, I've avoided her. I was afraid—" she paused to gain control over her emotions. "I'm very much like her. And I thought if I didn't come home, didn't do things she did, I wouldn't end up like her."

"Oh, Diane," Katie said softly. "Of course you're like her, in some ways. We all are. But we've got some of Dad in us, too. I always thought you were a great mixture. You have Dad's brain and Mom's heart. The best of both.

"Besides, Mom was born in a different time, as was Dad. Nowadays, women participate in life. Stay-at-home moms as well as working moms know how to care for themselves. Today, women get to make their own choices. It wasn't that way when Mom married."

Diane shook her head, fighting tears. "Don't make me feel worse, Katie. I didn't do anything to help. I didn't want to come back home."

Katie smiled. "You paid more of your schooling

than any of the others, holding a full-time job. You even sent back money occasionally.''

''That's so I wouldn't have to come back home,'' Diane confessed, a guilty secret she'd carried for a long time.

''What else did you do?'' Katie asked.

''I—I decided I'd never marry or have children. I'd concentrate on my career, so I'd never be dependent on anyone. I'd be strong.''

''You are strong. Strong enough, with the right man, to have it all without being weak,'' Katie assured her. ''You did what you could to help us. And we've made it, Di! We're all here, healthy, able to have the extras, knowing that we can face life. And you did your share.''

Diane shook her head, closing her eyes.

''What's wrong?'' another voice intruded.

Diane was horrified to recognize her mother's voice. ''Mom!''

''Hi, Mom. Where's Rachel?'' Katie asked.

''Jack's taking care of her. You know how he dotes on her. I had to run an errand. What's going on?''

''Diane is afraid she let us down,'' Katie said. ''I was just reassuring her how much she helped. And how proud we are of her.''

''Why, of course we are. Fortunately, none of my children take after me,'' Margaret said with a rueful smile.

Diane stared at her mother, surprised.

Margaret put a hand on Diane's shoulder. ''You

thought I didn't know how useless I've been? I know, child. If it weren't for Katie—''

''Now, wait just a minute,'' Katie said, standing and hugging her mother. ''We've all worked together.''

''Yes, I've improved, thanks to you children and Jack, but I'm not proud of my past.''

''Oh, Mom!'' Diane exclaimed, standing and clutching her mother in a monstrous hug.

''Why, Diane, you haven't hugged me like that in years!'' Margaret exclaimed, staring at Katie over Diane's shoulder.

''I think,'' Katie began with a smile, ''Diane has finally come home, Mom. Maybe to stay.''

AFTER DIANE RETURNED to the office, she tried to concentrate on her work, but she had too much to think about. It had been a life-changing discussion this afternoon. Now she was free to make her choices based on her likes and dislikes.

Immersed in her thoughts, she almost didn't hear her phone ring.

''Oh, Diane,'' her friend Sherry exclaimed, as soon as she answered. ''You should be glad you broke up with that Tom. He is such a jerk!''

''Oh, yeah?'' Diane replied. *Didn't she know it.*

''He got married two years ago. And his wife got pregnant at once.''

Right on schedule, Diane thought.

''Then, after the baby was born, he wouldn't help her at all. When she complained, he filed for divorce. Doesn't want to pay any support. The poor thing is living with her parents. And she was so young, a freshman. She's not trained to do anything.''

Just like her mother, except her dad had loved her and didn't abandon her by choice. ''When was the divorce final?''

''Oh, it's not. She's been fighting for child support that he doesn't want to pay. Aren't you glad he's out of your life?''

''Oh, yes. Thanks, Sherry. I'll come into Lubbock soon and buy you lunch. I definitely owe you.''

After she hung up, Diane tried to concentrate on work. But the emotional talk with her sister and mother had exhausted Diane, though she felt stronger and freer than she had in years.

She was pleased when the end of the workday arrived and she could head home. Then she remembered that Jeff wasn't going to be there when she arrived. All she'd been able to think about was telling Jeff what she'd decided. It was quite a let-down to come home to Thomas Westerby.

Why? She suddenly wondered why she hadn't protested his presence before. It wasn't like she had any interest in the man. And with the news Sherry had given her, she found nothing to admire in his behavior. With a grim smile, she made a decision. The man would not interfere in her life any longer. Jeff might be his host, but *she* was going to get rid of him. She'd told herself she was strong. It was time to let Thomas know that.

Her day suddenly brightened. When she reached the house, she got out of her car and marched inside. Both Hannah and Thomas met her as she came in. Thomas began his complaints, protesting her spending her day away from him. She calmly smiled.

"You're right, Thomas. I did spend my day away from you. And will continue to do so. It's time you left. I'm sure you're missing work and for no reason."

"Of course it's for a reason. I need to get my life back on track. I need you," he assured her with a frown.

"But I don't need you, and no matter what you think, there's nothing you can do that will convince me, because, you see, I'm…interested in someone else…permanently. So I suggest you go pack your bags and head back to Lubbock. You have plenty of time to drive and get a good night's sleep in your own place."

"Who? Who are you interested in?"

Diane looked at Hannah's attentive stare. Hoping to make her think she wasn't serious, she smiled at the housekeeper before saying to Thomas, "The doctor, of course. I can't resist the lure of free medical care for the rest of my life."

"Quit teasing, Diane. He's too old for you. With me, you'd have a lot of fun. We could travel like you've always wanted, live in a sophisticated city, have excitement in our lives. You said that's what you wanted when you turned me down the last time. Is the doctor willing to give up having children?"

"I hope not," she said with a soft smile. "I really hope not."

"Of course he'll want children," Hannah said, smiling, too. "Babies are a precious gift, and you and Dr. Jeff will make the most beautiful babies."

"Wait a minute. What's going on here? You don't want children."

"Yes, I do, Thomas. I've changed. So have you, but not in the same direction. I have no interest in you or how you live your life. I just want you out of mine. Go pack."

"You can't throw me out!"

"Yes, I can. And if you refuse to go, I'll call the sheriff and have *him* throw you out." She only hoped Thomas didn't know that Cal was with Jeff. But she was pretty sure his deputies would help her even if Cal was unavailable. "Those would be great headlines in Lubbock. 'Thomas Westerby Arrested.'"

She loved the fear that filled his eyes. Thomas never wanted bad publicity. What mattered to him was his reputation. Love was an emotion he didn't understand.

"You wouldn't do that!" he protested.

The look on Hannah's face told Diane the housekeeper didn't think she would either, and Thomas had noticed that. With a chuckle, Diane walked to the phone and lifted the receiver. Then she dialed the number for Cal's office. She'd known the receptionist all her life. "Betty, I need to have someone thrown out of Jeff's house. He won't leave. Can someone help me?''

''No!'' Thomas yelled and pushed down the button, ending the call.

Paul came into the kitchen. ''What's going on?''

Toby and Janie followed him, staring at the adults.

''I asked Thomas to leave and he refused, so I called the sheriff's office for some help.'' Diane still had her hand on the receiver when it rang. She answered and heard a calm voice. ''Hon, this is Betty. Do you want me to send someone?''

''Yes, please.'' Then she hung up the phone. ''You'd better hurry, Thomas. They'll be here in about two minutes.''

''I can't believe you'd—they can't arrest me! I haven't done anything wrong!''

''Well, Cal's not actually there, so they'll just put you in jail and wait until he comes in the morning. But it doesn't matter to me because my problem will be solved. You'll be gone.'' She smiled at him. Hannah also was smiling, but Paul was frowning.

''You don't need to call someone. I can throw him out.''

Thomas pushed out his chest. ''Oh, yeah? You and who else?'' Thomas wasn't weak. He worked out in a gym in Lubbock. A sophisticated gym where important people worked out. Diane hadn't wanted to risk her brother in a fight.

''I know, Paul, but I really don't want a brawl. Let the law take care of him.''

Thomas started to protest again, but someone knocked on the back door. His eyes widened and he turned around to head for the stairs.

Diane answered the back door to greet Pete, one of Cal's deputies.

"Hi, Diane. You got problems?"

"Yeah. I think your arrival will take care of it, if you'll just hang around for a minute. Hannah, can you offer Pete a cup of coffee?"

"I'll even cut him a piece of cake, if he wants it," Hannah agreed with a smile. "Getting rid of that man would be more than worth it."

"Who are we getting rid of?" the deputy asked as he sat down at the table.

"Thomas Westerby," Diane readily said. "I asked him to leave and he refused. Can we charge him with trespassing? Or harassment? Or something?"

Pete shrugged. "I'm sure we can find something. How's the doc feel about it? Is this man a personal friend of his?"

Before Diane could answer, Hannah said, "He hates him. He only invited him to stay because he said he was a friend of Diane's. I'm sure he'll be pleased if he's gone…so they can get on with more important things." She beamed at Diane.

"What more important things?" Pete asked.

Diane choked on her own breath when she saw Hannah open her mouth, happy to inform the deputy about what she thought Diane and Jeff would do— once they were alone.

Chapter Sixteen

Jeff had untied one athletic shoe and toed it off before he reached the bed. He sat down to remove the second shoe. Then he ripped off his shirt. He didn't bother hanging it up. He was too tired for that. Tossing it on the floor, he stood and reached for the buttons on his jeans. Then he realized he hadn't re-closed his door, and staggered over to shut it. Exhaustion and sore muscles kept him focused on reaching the bed and falling down face first. He undid his jeans and slid them down his muscular legs, then shoved off his socks. He again crossed the room and snapped off the light.

Finally, he could close his eyes.

He rolled into the bed, pulling the covers over him. He slept in the middle of the bed and he automatically scooted over...until he brushed against warm flesh.

As tired as he was, Jeff still knew no one should be in his bed. And it didn't take gigantic intelligence to know that the person in his bed was Diane.

He could smell her perfume. He didn't know why she was there. But he gave thanks that he could hold her once more.

He'd told himself he shouldn't touch her again. They had no future. They didn't want the same things. It would be wrong to use her for his pleasure when he knew they didn't have the same goals. But damn, she felt good.

Ending his debate, going with his baser need, he gathered her into his arms. His lips touched hers. He only intended to kiss her awake and ask what she was doing there, he told himself. But when her lips moved under his, the blood flow picked up and his heart began racing.

She pushed against his chest and he reluctantly pulled away.

"Jeff! You're back!" she exclaimed, pleasure in her voice, as well as sleepiness.

"Yeah," he agreed, wondering if he could have one more kiss before she disappeared.

"I need you—"

Like a sprinter given the go-ahead, he leaped forward, his lips covering hers, his hands reaching for her warm skin. He'd dreamed about making love to Diane again. He'd told himself that it wouldn't be as thrilling, as pleasurable as it had been the first time. But he'd still dreamed of it.

Now he knew why. The reality—if it was reality—was even better than the first time.

It did surprise him to discover Diane was dressed

in shorts and T-shirt rather than silk. In his dreams she'd always worn silk.

"Di, I was afraid—" he pulled back to say, trying to express his thoughts. But there was no doubt of Diane's desire. It appeared to match his. She willingly helped him remove her clothes, then added his briefs to the pile on the floor.

"Jeff." Diane ran her hands over his body as he abandoned her mouth to pay attention to other parts of Diane's body.

"Yes, oh, yes!" he muttered and returned his mouth to hers. He couldn't get enough of her, but the building tension in his body told him going slow and easy still wasn't an option.

She didn't seem to mind his urgency. In fact, she encouraged him. He wanted to explain that he couldn't get enough of her. Next time he'd go slower. Next time. What a wonderful thought that he'd have a next time with Diane.

Diane couldn't believe she could lose control so quickly. But the man was incredible. It only took one touch for him to set her on fire. She'd had plans to explain her presence in his bed. It had gotten late. She hadn't wanted to miss talking to him. She'd figured he'd be curious about her presence in his bed. He'd wake her up and they'd discuss—

Okay, okay, she'd hoped they'd make love. She felt guilty about it, so she'd kept on her shorts and T-shirt. But this is what she'd wanted. A moan of pleasure escaped her mouth.

His lips returned to hers and she didn't care about

anything. Just Jeff. Tomorrow they'd talk. Tomorrow she'd tell him her goals had changed. She could tell him that Thomas was gone. She could tell him...that she loved him...tomorrow.

A KNOCKING ON A DOOR somewhere awoke Diane. It was probably for Jeff, she decided. He'd get it. Besides, she was too comfortable, too satisfied, too warm in Jeff's arms.

In Jeff's arms.

That phrase slowly penetrated Diane's head. Flashes of yesterday, her calling Cal's office to get rid of Tom, her shameful entry into Jeff's bed. She'd planned to talk to him before she seduced him. But he'd been willing, more than willing, so she'd postponed the conversation until morning. Until now.

She poked him. When he opened his eyes, she said, "I need to talk to you about the current situation of the house."

Jeff got out of bed, looking more than a little confused, and pulled on his briefs. He turned to face her. "What situation?"

Diane pressed her lips together, tried to gather her thoughts. "I, uh, asked Tom to leave. He refused, but—I convinced him to go." She didn't see any need to mention Pete's arrival. "I know it's your house, but I couldn't stand having him here. He was upsetting the kids."

Jeff, his gaze still fastened on her face, nodded slowly. "I'm glad he's gone, frankly. He annoyed me."

"Was that the reason you were avoiding us?" she couldn't help asking. She knew she had more to ask him. But she finally admitted to herself she was scared. Scared that he didn't want her for anything but sex.

Jeff looked away. "Avoid you? Don't be ridiculous," he said, but he still didn't look at her.

Her heart sank. He didn't want her.

With the sheet wrapped around her body, she came around the bed to gather her discarded clothes into her arms.

"Diane," Jeff began.

Hope flooded her. Did he want her? Could she find happiness in his arms? Her emotions were like a rollercoaster. But she wanted Jeff's love.

Another knock disturbed them. But this time it wasn't on Jeff's door, but the back door.

Jeff ran his fingers through his hair and looked at the clock beside his bed. "It's not even eight o'clock. Who could that be? Thomas?"

She stiffened. "Are you hoping it is?"

"Damn it, no. I'm glad he's gone."

"I'll dress and go downstairs. You can stay in bed since you—you got in late."

She hurried out the door closing it behind her. Why not answer the door. Maybe it would be someone who wanted to talk to her. The man in bed clearly didn't.

Jeff might not know what to say, but he figured he'd better think fast. He grabbed the jeans he'd thrown on the floor last night and put them on. Then he pulled on a clean T-shirt and ran for the stairs.

He burst into the kitchen to see Cal sitting with Paul and the kids.

"You're going to have breakfast with us?" Toby asked, a hopeful look in his eyes that made Jeff feel guilty.

"Uh, yeah, son, I'm having breakfast with you."

Before he could ask any questions, Paul told him to sit down and fixed him a plate of eggs and bacon.

"Uh, hasn't your sister come down?" Jeff asked after Paul sat down again. "She was going to come answer the door."

"She's always slow," Paul said with a grin.

"I heard that!" Diane snapped as she entered the kitchen. She stopped suddenly when she realized Cal was there. "Oh, hi, Cal. What are you doing here?"

"Having some coffee. I didn't know young Paul knew how to make such good coffee. I may have to start coming here in the morning."

"I've got a better idea. You should hire him to come over and make your coffee."

"I'll think about it. Actually, I wanted to check on everything here, make sure you're not still having problems."

No one answered. Jeff looked first at Paul, then Diane.

Finally he asked, "Problems? No one mentioned any problems. Especially not anything serious enough to call the sheriff's office."

Paul looked at his sister. So did Cal. So Jeff knew who had the answer to his unspoken question. He stared at her, too, waiting.

She kept her gaze on the table. When she looked up, it was to ask Paul to take the children into the den.

"But I wanted to have breakfast with Dr. Jeff," Toby complained.

Jeff quickly said, "I'm going to be home all morning. We'll play cars in a little while." He knew he wasn't going to get any answers until the children were out of the way. How did married couples ever manage to talk? Maybe they did that in bed at night.

Once the other three were out of the room, Diane took a deep breath and said, "Thomas refused to leave. He said Jeff was his host and I couldn't make him leave. I was worried about Paul fighting with him, so I decided to call for help. I didn't want him here anymore."

"Me, either," Jeff said.

Cal said, "I can understand that."

Both men chuckled.

"Pete said he didn't even have to say anything," Cal added.

"No, Thomas has a rabid fear of bad publicity," Diane explained.

"Well, if he comes back, don't expect me to be friendly to him. I don't want him in my house again."

"Surely you don't think I would invite him?" Diane said, a hint of outrage in her voice.

"From what I hear, you two will be too busy to—"

"Cal!" Diane exclaimed in a frantic voice.

Jeff stared at Cal's amused expression to Diane's panic. He kept his gaze on Diane. "What's he talking about?" he asked, nodding in Cal's direction.

She didn't look at him, but she did answer. "It was s-stuff I made up to convince Thomas to leave. Pete must've thought I meant it."

"Oh, sorry, Diane. I'd hoped—well, I'll try to squash the rumor." Cal stood, but Diane didn't want him to go yet.

"Who did Pete tell?"

"Just a couple of my deputies. They'd talked about—" he stopped and cleared his throat. "You know—your availability." He moved to the door. "Glad everything's okay here."

Neither spoke after Cal's departure. Finally Jeff said, "Didn't you think you should tell me you'd called for help?"

"I intended to—last night. I just didn't get to it. And I haven't had a chance to since I woke up."

Guilt filled Jeff. She was blaming his lovemaking for his lack of information. And she was right.

Diane felt guilty. It wasn't fair to blame Jeff. She'd intended to seduce him. She'd thought she could talk first. But she was the one who'd let things get out of hand.

"I'm sorry. I shouldn't—"

"No, you're right." He cleared his throat. "You're going to have to leave, Diane."

Diane's heart fell. She'd hoped to talk to Jeff about what had happened last night, explain how things had changed, how much she loved him. Though it appeared he'd already made up his mind about them.

But she wasn't a quitter.

"Why?" she asked softly.

"Because that can't happen again. And I can't promise I can keep my hands off you. You're—you're very attractive."

"You mean because we didn't use protection?" she asked. That thought had occurred to her when Cal had started talking about what she'd told Thomas. She hadn't panicked, however. She loved Jeff.

Something flared in his eyes so briefly she couldn't be sure what it was. Then he pulled himself together to say, "I apologize. I was so tired last night and I didn't expect—I'll raise the child if—if there is one. It won't affect your plans."

Diane stared at him. He thought she'd abandon her own child? What was wrong with the man? It was going to be hard enough to let go of Toby and Janie when Evie was ready to take them. But he thought she'd give up a child that grew inside her for nine months? *His* child?

"You'll do no such thing!" she shouted.

"Di, I want—I'll take good care of him. I won't bother you for anything, but—"

"I'm a lawyer. I'll fight you in any court in the

world before I'd give my child away. You can't make me.''

"You don't want to—I mean, you'd keep the baby?''

"Of course!''

"But a big city isn't a good place to keep a child. I've already got Hannah, and I'd be close by. And— and you said Cactus is a good place to raise a child.''

Diane was feeling light-headed. Too much adrenaline this morning. She was becoming confused. "I didn't say— Why are we arguing? We don't even know— I'll go pack.''

She hurried up the stairs, pulling out the duffel bag she kept in the back of the closet. She guessed she could sleep on the sofa at Katie's. She didn't think Jeff intended to let her take the children with her. He'd just get Hannah to come in earlier.

She was too distracted to hear quiet footsteps behind her.

"Diane?''

She spun around, almost losing her balance, to stare at Jeff. "W-What?

"You didn't come to my room last night to seduce me, did you?''

That was a question Diane didn't want to answer. But she couldn't be less than honest with this man. "Yes. Yes, I did. It's not your fault. I wanted to talk first, but I wanted—I'd hoped you'd want to—want me.''

He sighed. "I guess I don't have to tell you that you were right, do I?"

She shook her head but said nothing.

"Why don't you tell me now what you wanted to say?"

"I—I made a big discovery."

"You did?" he asked, his eyebrows rising.

"It's a long story but the abbreviated version is I got confused. I'd been sure for so long that I didn't want marriage or children. But I love Janie and Toby, which didn't make sense. And I was enjoying taking care of everyone. I started questioning myself. I talked to Katie and Mom. Then I finally began to understand where my fears stemmed from. I didn't want to be a housewife because that was what Mom had been. And she'd been lost when Dad died."

He still looked puzzled.

She hurried on. "I didn't want to be weak, like Mom. But I realized that here in Cactus, I could be a lawyer and a wife and mother, like Alexandra. I could have it all!"

"And that's what you want?" he asked, doubt in his voice.

"Oh, yes. If—if you're the one asking."

He moved closer. "Let me be sure I'm getting this right. You think marrying me would give you a happy life, children and all?"

"Even a dog. A perfect family."

He pulled her into his arms, his lips covering hers.

She thought everything was settled, but when he stepped back, she still saw questions in his gaze.

"Why? Why are you ready to settle in Cactus? You wanted excitement, travel."

He needed more reassurance? She could give him that. "Because I love you! My day is exciting if I can start it with you. And end it with you. I love my job. And I want to have your babies. That doesn't mean I wouldn't mind an occasional trip. But once a year should be enough, as long as you're with me."

"But, honey, are you sure?"

"I love you, Jeff, but if—if you don't feel the same, we can—"

Once more he embraced her, this time the kiss longer and deeper. "I guess I forgot to mention that I can't breathe if you're not in my life. I love you more than life itself."

"Very nicely said," she returned with a beaming smile. "Let's go back to bed. I didn't get enough time with you this morning," she suggested.

"But the children— Okay, let me go bribe Paul, and I'll be right back. Do I know where to find you?"

"Oh, yes. I'll be waiting."

BETWEEN DISCUSSIONS THAT night in bed, Jeff made love to Diane. By the time they rose the next morning, they were in desperate need of sleep.

When Paul came into the kitchen, he stared at

both of them. "Didn't you get any sleep last night either?"

Diane blushed and Jeff cleared his throat. "Uh, Paul, I have something to tell you."

"Yeah?" he asked as he poured himself a giant glass of milk from the fridge. "What? Don't tell me that jerk is coming back."

"Nope. I can promise you won't ever see him in my house again," Jeff said. "But, uh, I'm going to marry your sister."

Paul stared at them in stunned silence. Just when Diane decided she should say something, Paul yelled, "Wow! That's terrific! Welcome to the family, Jeff!"

They received the same reaction as they phoned Katie and her mother. Then Jeff called his friends in Cactus. Cal seemed the least surprised. As soon as eight o'clock came, he called his office and discovered he only had four appointments that morning. He asked his nurse to reschedule them and told her he'd be in at noon.

"I should've asked Hannah to come in early," he muttered.

"Why? Go back upstairs and take a nap," Diane suggested.

"A nap?" Toby asked, a look of horror on his face. "I just got up."

"A nap for Dr. Jeff," Diane explained.

Before anyone else could speak, the doorbell rang.

Diane peeked out the window. "It's Mabel and

Florence. And Edith and Ruth, too. Why would they— Oh, dear. Cactus gossip.''

She escorted the ladies into the kitchen for a cup of coffee.

''Congratulations, we heard the news,'' Mabel announced as she sat down.

''How surprising,'' Diane teased.

''Well, we should've waited, but we had a wonderful idea,'' Florence said, beaming.

''Okay,'' Jeff said, dragging out the two syllables. ''What?''

''We want you to get married on July fourth, as part of the festival,'' Florence responded.

Jeff immediately opened his mouth to refuse, but Ruth beat him to the punch.

''You see, you could leave on your honeymoon at the end of the day, and Evie could move into your house, with Hannah to take care of her and the kids while you're gone. By the time you get back, she'll be able to live on her own. We've found the cutest little house just across the street from me, so I can keep an eye on her. Isn't that wonderful?''

Diane stared at Jeff, and he read the response in her eyes. They'd discussed some wedding plans, but they hadn't made up their minds. But he was all in favor of doing it soon.

''Can you manage that quickly, Di?'' he asked.

''Oh, we can help her,'' Edith said. ''We're old hands at weddings.''

''And since we're responsible, we thought we *should* help.'' Mabel grinned like a cheshire cat.

"I thought you were trying to marry her off to Westerby. No fair to claim matchmaking between the two of us."

"Oh, yes we can," Mabel assured him. "Well, sort of. I pushed you into inviting that horrible man because it would make you realize you loved Diane. So we can put another notch in our bedposts. This romance is a Cactus special!"

The other ladies cheered and Jeff found himself and Diane cheering along with them. Why not? He'd never been happier.

Epilogue

July Fourth dawned with the promise of a beautiful day. Not too hot, the bright sunshine combined with a pleasant breeze. Diane had spent the night at her mother's newly-repaired house and had missed Jeff terribly.

Jeff had been at his house...and his bed had felt empty without Diane. Paul had spent the night at Jeff's to get him to the church on time. The prime duty for the best man.

Everyone else in town was up early to prepare for the carnival *and* the wedding. Word had spread that casual dress was expected at the occasion. In fact, everything had gone so smoothly it was scary. They'd allowed the experts, the four matchmakers, to run the show.

Diane greeted the day with breakfast served in bed. Or on the couch, with her mother and three sisters.

"I was going to ask if you were sure about this," Raine said, "but since you've been smiling like a woman in paradise ever since I got here, I guess I don't need to.''

"Nope," Diane agreed. "I've never been happier, except I miss Jeff.''

"Twelve hours apart and she's complaining?" Raine asked. "Isn't that weird?"

Katie laughed quietly. "I completely understand."

"Me, too," their mother agreed.

Raine stared at them. "I think I'd better get out of town before I catch the same bug. I certainly don't intend to act like y'all."

"We'll see," Diane said. "I'm ready to get dressed and go to the festival. I hope it's a big success."

"You're actually going to try to pop balloons or do the cakewalk before you put on your wedding gown?"

"Well, I don't think I should wear my gown *before* the wedding." Diane assured her younger sister, Susan. "So let's go."

CROWDS WERE IN THE square by nine o'clock. Huge crowds for Cactus. It looked like the best turnout ever. Diane saw Evie, proudly escorted by Toby and Janie, almost as soon as she arrived. With a shout, she hurried over to them. "Evie! How are you feeling?"

"Just fine, Diane. How's the bride?"

Diane blushed. She loved being called a bride.

"Fine. If you get tired, Paul said he'd take you over to our house."

"I know. Everyone's being so nice. Did I tell you Mabel found me a job? Next month I'm going to be an assistant manager at the grocery store. I'll be making good money and the hours are while the kids are in school. I can't believe it!"

"I told you Cactus is a great place to live."

"Diane!" Melanie, Spence's wife, called, waving Diane over. "Have you entered the raffle? It's for an Oriental rug. I bet you could use one in your new home. Dr. Jeff didn't bring a lot of furniture with him from Houston."

"You're right. Of course, I'll enter." She knew, as did the rest of the town, that the raffle was rigged. Evie would win the rug. And the money would go to her account.

"May I enter?" Evie asked. "The sign says only one dollar."

Diane and Melanie exchanged a grin. "Of course you can," Melanie agreed. "We're going to have the raffle just before the wedding."

Evie frowned. "You're not waiting until the end of the day? You'd sell more tickets if you waited."

"Oh, we've been selling them at my store for a week. We have plenty of entries. See you then."

"I have to go to the dunking booth. Jeff is taking the first shift and I want to dunk him," Diane said as she and Evie, along with the children, walked away.

Since she'd been on the softball team in high

school, Diane gathered a crowd as she approached the booth where Jeff sat on a collapsible seat. Jeff's eyes widened as he realized his beautiful bride was picking up a ball.

"Sweetheart," she called. "Here's your wedding present."

As the crowd laughed, she threw a perfect strike and sent him splashing into the tank below. He'd barely gotten up and back on his seat when the second ball arrived, repeating the process.

"Hey, lady, you're going to pay for that! Tonight I'll have you in my clutches!"

"I know!" she cooed. "And I can't wait!"

The crowd roared with laughter and rushed forward to have their own try at the happy groom.

Jeff only hoped they weren't as accurate as his bride.

WHEN THE BAND began the Wedding March, the booths were empty and the guests were seated in folding chairs. A few were stretched out on the grass. Diane had changed into her wedding garb, a sleeveless satin gown, with pearls sewn around the rounded neckline and others scattered on the A-line skirt. In its simplicity, Diane looked like an angel in Jeff's mind. His only objection was the veil that half-hid her sweet face from view.

But within minutes, he pulled back the veil to kiss his new wife. Her beauty was breathtaking, but he loved her in a sweatshirt and jeans just as much. In fact, he loved her however she appeared.

"I love you," he whispered in her ear before he turned her to face their friends and neighbors as the minister introduced them as Dr. and Mrs. Hausen. Diane kissed him again before she faced the audience, whispering "I love you" in his ear.

"Cut it out, guys," Paul leaned over and whispered. "That's for later."

"That's for always," Diane said as she grinned at her husband and her brother.

The next half hour they visited with their friends, ate a little barbeque, and smiled constantly. Then they cut the huge wedding cake Katie had made for them. After the first piece was cut, Ruth took over slicing pieces with her partners-in-matchmaking assisting her by passing out the pieces.

"You're through now, dears," Mabel said. "Have a happy honeymoon."

Jeff whispered to Diane, "Get changed. We've got a plane to catch."

Diane didn't hesitate. She was anxious to be with her husband. She appeared five minutes later in a new suit she'd bought for the occasion. A limo was waiting, much to her surprise. "A limo? Where are we going?"

Jeff had insisted on keeping their destination a secret. Not that she cared as long as they were together.

He refused to answer, and found other things to do while the limo drove them into Lubbock. Then they got on a plane to Dallas.

"Do I get to shop in Dallas?" Diane asked. Dallas was known for its shopping.

"We're not stopping there, though I think I may have made a mistake."

"What kind of mistake?" she asked as she buckled her seat belt.

"I didn't schedule a layover there. Our first night as newlyweds is going to be spent on a plane," Jeff said, grinning at her.

"All night? But where—where are we going?"

"You wanted excitement and travel. We're going to London and Paris," he said proudly.

"Oh, Jeff!" she exclaimed. "How—how exciting…and thoughtful. You're so wonderful."

"I wanted you to know you could have it all with me," he said tenderly, pulling her into his arms and kissing her.

After he released her, she reached up to stroke his cheek. "I never doubted it, Jeff. As long as I have you, I already have it all."

* * * * *

Don't miss Judy Christenberry's next
Harlequin American Romance.

RANDALL PRIDE

will be on sale
this August.

USA Today bestselling author

STELLA CAMERON

and popular American Romance author

MURIEL JENSEN

come together in a special
Harlequin 2-in-1 collection.

Look for

Shadows and *Daddy in Demand*

On sale June 2001

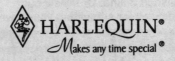

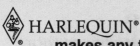

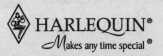

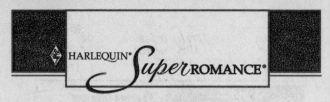

HARLEQUIN *Super*ROMANCE®

To celebrate the
1000th Superromance book
We're presenting you with 3 books
from 3 of your favorite authors in

All Summer Long

Home, Hearth and Haley
by **Muriel Jensen**

Meet the men and women of Muriel's
upcoming **Men of Maple Hill** trilogy

Daddy's Girl
by **Judith Arnold**

Another **Daddy School** story!

Temperature Rising
by **Bobby Hutchinson**

Life and love at St. Joe's Hospital are as feverish
as ever in this **Emergency!** story

On sale July 2001
Available wherever Harlequin books are sold.

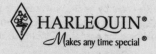

HARLEQUIN®
Makes any time special ®

HSR1000

HARLEQUIN WALK DOWN THE AISLE TO MAUI CONTEST 1197
OFFICIAL RULES
NO PURCHASE NECESSARY TO ENTER

1. To enter, follow directions published in the offer to which you are responding. Contest begins April 2, 2001, and ends on October 1, 2001. Method of entry may vary. Mailed entries must be postmarked by October 1, 2001, and received by October 8, 2001.

2. Contest entry may be, at times, presented via the Internet, but will be restricted solely to residents of certain geographic areas that are disclosed on the Web site. To enter via the Internet, if permissible, access the Harlequin Web site (www.eHarlequin.com) and follow the directions displayed online. Online entries must be received by 11:59 p.m. E.S.T. on October 1, 2001.

   In lieu of submitting an entry online, enter by mail by hand-printing (or typing) on an 8½" x 11" plain piece of paper, your name, address (including zip code), Contest number/name and in 250 words or fewer, why winning a Harlequin wedding dre would make your wedding day special. Mail via first-class mail to: Harlequin Walk Down the Aisle Contest 1197, (in the U.S P.O. Box 9076, 3010 Walden Avenue, Buffalo, NY 14269-9076, (in Canada) P.O. Box 637, Fort Erie, Ontario L2A 5X3, Canad

   Limit one entry per person, household address and e-mail address. Online and/or mailed entries received from persons residing in geographic areas in which Internet entry is not permissible will be disqualified.

3. Contests will be judged by a panel of members of the Harlequin editorial, marketing and public relations staff based on the following criteria:

   - Originality and Creativity—50%
   - Emotionally Compelling—25%
   - Sincerity—25%

   In the event of a tie, duplicate prizes will be awarded. Decisions of the judges are final.

4. All entries become the property of Torstar Corp. and will not be returned. No responsibility is assumed for lost, late, illegible incomplete, inaccurate, nondelivered or misdirected mail or misdirected e-mail, for technical, hardware or software failures o any kind, lost or unavailable network connections, or failed, incomplete, garbled or delayed computer transmission or any human error which may occur in the receipt or processing of the entries in this Contest.

5. Contest open only to residents of the U.S. (except Puerto Rico) and Canada, who are 18 years of age or older, and is void wherever prohibited by law; all applicable laws and regulations apply. Any litigation within the Province of Quebec respecting the conduct or organization of a publicity contest may be submitted to the Régie des alcools, des courses et des jeux for a ruling. Any litigation respecting the awarding of a prize may be submitted to the Régie des alcools, des courses et des jeux o for the purpose of helping the parties reach a settlement. Employees and immediate family members of Torstar Corp. and D. L. Blair, Inc., their affiliates, subsidiaries and all other agencies, entities and persons connected with the use, marketing or conduct of this Contest are not eligible to enter. Taxes on prizes are the sole responsibility of winners. Acceptance of any priz offered constitutes permission to use winner's name, photograph or other likeness for the purposes of advertising, trade and promotion on behalf of Torstar Corp., its affiliates and subsidiaries without further compensation to the winner, unless prohibited by law.

6. Winners will be determined no later than November 15, 2001, and will be notified by mail. Winners will be required to sign a return the Affidavit of Eligibility form within 15 days after winner notification. Noncompliance within that time period may resul in disqualification and an alternative winner may be selected. Winners of trip must execute a Release of Liability prior to ticket and must possess required travel documents (e.g. passport, photo ID) where applicable. Trip must be completed by November 2002. No substitution of prize permitted by winner. Torstar Corp. and D. L. Blair, Inc., their parents, affiliates, and subsidiaries are not responsible for errors in printing or electronic presentation of Contest, entries and/or game pieces. In the event of printing or other errors which may result in unintended prize values or duplication of prizes, all affected game pieces or entrie shall be null and void. If for any reason the Internet portion of the Contest is not capable of running as planned, including infection by computer virus, bugs, tampering, unauthorized intervention, fraud, technical failures, or any other causes beyond the control of Torstar Corp. which corrupt or affect the administration, secrecy, fairness, integrity or proper conduct of the Contest, Torstar Corp. reserves the right, at its sole discretion, to disqualify any individual who tampers with the entry process and to cancel, terminate, modify or suspend the Contest or the Internet portion thereof. In the event of a dispute regarding an online entry, the entry will be deemed submitted by the authorized holder of the e-mail account submitted at the time of entry. Authorized account holder is defined as the natural person who is assigned to an e-mail address by an Internet access provid online service provider or other organization that is responsible for arranging e-mail address for the domain associated with t submitted e-mail address. **Purchase or acceptance of a product offer does not improve your chances of winnin**

7. Prizes: (1) Grand Prize—A Harlequin wedding dress (approximate retail value: $3,500) and a 5-night/6-day honeymoon trip Maui, HI, including round-trip air transportation provided by Maui Visitors Bureau from Los Angeles International Airport (winner is responsible for transportation to and from Los Angeles International Airport) and a Harlequin Romance Package, including hotel accomodations (double occupancy) at the Hyatt Regency Maui Resort and Spa, dinner for (2) two at Swan Court, a sunset sail on Kiele V and a spa treatment for the winner (approximate retail value: $4,000); (5) Five runner-up prize of a $1000 gift certificate to selected retail outlets to be determined by Sponsor (retail value $1000 ea.). Prizes consist of only those items listed as part of the prize. Limit one prize per person. All prizes are valued in U.S. currency.

8. For a list of winners (available after December 17, 2001) send a self-addressed, stamped envelope to: Harlequin Walk Down Aisle Contest 1197 Winners, P.O. Box 4200 Blair, NE 68009-4200 or you may access the www.eHarlequin.com Web site through January 15, 2002.

Contest sponsored by Torstar Corp., P.O. Box 9042, Buffalo, NY 14269-9042, U.S.A.

PHWDACONT2

Harlequin truly does
make any time special. . . .
This year we are celebrating
weddings in style!

A
Walk
Down
the Aisle

WEDDING CELEBRATION

To help us celebrate, we want you to tell us how wearing the
Harlequin wedding gown will make your wedding day special. As
the grand prize, Harlequin will offer one lucky bride the chance to
"Walk Down the Aisle" in the Harlequin wedding gown!

There's more...

For her honeymoon, she and her groom will spend five nights at the
Hyatt Regency Maui. As part of this five-night honeymoon at the
hotel renowned for its romantic attractions, the couple will enjoy a candlelit
dinner for two in Swan Court, a sunset sail on the hotel's catamaran, and
duet spa treatments.

Maui • Molokai • Lanai

To enter, please write, in, 250 words or less, how wearing the Harlequin
wedding gown will make your wedding day special. The entry will be
judged based on its emotionally compelling nature, its originality and
creativity, and its sincerity. This contest is open to Canadian and U.S.
residents only and to those who are 18 years of age and older. There is no
purchase necessary to enter. Void where prohibited. See further contest
rules attached. Please send your entry to:

Walk Down the Aisle Contest

In Canada	In U.S.A.
P.O. Box 637	P.O. Box 9076
Fort Erie, Ontario	3010 Walden Ave.
L2A 5X3	Buffalo, NY 14269-9076

You can also enter by visiting www.eHarlequin.com
Win the Harlequin wedding gown and the vacation of a lifetime!
The deadline for entries is October 1, 2001.

HARLEQUIN®
Makes any time special ®

PHWDACONT1